'The Cheerake tell us, that when they first arrived in the country which they inhabit, they found it possessed by certain moon-eyed people, who could not see in the day-time. These wretches they expelled.'

Benjamin Smith Barton, New Views of the Origin of the Tribes and Nations of America, 1797.

•◆•

'I have heard my grandfather and other old people say, that they were a people called Welsh ... a Frenchman, who lived with the Cherokees ... informed me, 'that he had been high up the Missouri, and traded several months with the Welsh tribe; that they spoke much of the Welsh dialect, and although their customs were savage and wild, yet many of them, particularly the females were very fair and white, and frequently told him, they had sprung from a white nation of people; also stated they had yet some small scraps of books remaining among them, but in such tattered and destructive order, that nothing intelligible remained.'

John Sevier, Governor of Tennessee, letter to Amos Stoddard, 9 October 1810.

Contents

Introduction

Alone man wanders from swamp to swamp searching for himself, an owl remembers she was once human, a woman is in love with two moons, a war over land enclosures leads to mass migration, a skunk chases a greedy bear from his home, a wolf-girl visits Wales and eats the sheep, a Brecon preacher walks on the Trail of Tears, Welsh weavers make cloth for enslaved people, a mining settlement in Appalachia is described as being unfit for pigs, a spear-fingered monster is defeated with menstrual blood, a Welsh criminal marries an 'Indian Princess', Lakota men who witnessed Wounded Knee re-enact the massacre in Cardiff, and all the while mountain women practise Appalachian hoodoo, native healing, and Welsh witchcraft.

These stories are a mixture of true tales, tall tales and folk tales that tell of the lives of migrants who left west Wales and settled in and around Appalachia, of the native people who were already living on the land, the enslaved people who had been forcibly brought there, and those curious travellers who returned to their roots in the old country. They were explorers, farmers, hunters, miners, dreamers, hobos, radicals, showmen, singers, sailors, soldiers, storytellers, liars, witches, warriors, poets, preachers, tourists, colonists, political dissidents, social reformers, and wayfaring strangers.

Those who left Wales had little idea of what lay ahead for them. Benjamin Williams of Mynydd Bach in Ceredigion was about 17 when he sailed for America:

> Having sold the farm in the summer of 1838, we prepared to come to America ... we set out in carts from Lledrod to Aberayron: we were there for many days ... 175 Welsh people ready to embark for Liverpool in three sloops ... we had to wait a few days before boarding the sailing ship. People over 18 years paid £20; from 10 to 18 half-price, under five came free ... the doctor came aboard and examined us to see whether we were fit for the voyage and decided that many of the children weren't fit to sail ... Some ill people were hidden and when they were discovered it was too late to turn back ... 17 children, and all those under 10, died, great sadness, Rahel crying for her children. Six weeks of sailing through several storms; we lost the course for Baltimore and sailed towards Cuba before the elements subsided and we got back on to the correct course.

When the migrants landed in Baltimore or Boston, they were sometimes renamed by the immigration authorities, who couldn't pronounce or spell their real names. Those who spoke only Welsh were confronted with languages and dialects from Scotland, Ireland, England, Italy, Romania, Germany, Sweden, Hungary, Holland, Greece, Poland, Russia, Slovakia, Bohemia, French Canada, Latin America, and all parts of Africa and Asia. They crossed the endless ridges of the Allegheny Mountains with belongings tied to wagons and pack mules, and negotiated the purchase of land from companies who had taken it from people who already lived there.

Many of the Welsh settled in Pennsylvania, where they encountered the Shawnee, indigenous people who spoke an Algonquin language. From Pittsburgh, they moved down the Ohio and Monongahela Rivers through West Virginia into North Carolina, Kentucky, and Tennessee, the area known as Southern Appalachia.

Here they met the Aniyunwiya, who the colonists called Cherokee, a corruption of a native word meaning 'people who speak differently'. They called themselves Tsalagi, and told stories in an Iroquoian language, Tsalagi Gawonihisdi; tales the invaders couldn't begin to understand.

They encountered enslaved people and their descendants, brought over on boats against their will, packed like sardines in the cruellest conditions, bought and sold like cattle, prevented from speaking their own languages. These people told their stories in a Black English language based on the shared African belief in 'Nommo', the idea that a word when spoken was the power of life, and its beauty told an oral history of forced migration.

Folk tales in all cultures carry memories of migration. Peter Henry Emerson, son of an American plantation owner in Cuba, published a little-known story that was told to him near Menai Bridge, Ynys Môn, in 1891. It tells of how the ancestors of the Welsh escaped persecution and taxation in Persia, built a great city called Troy, made their way through feast and famine to Brittany, and over the water to Brython, where they were pushed ever westwards by successive invaders.

There are migration narratives in the fourteenth-century Llyfr Gwyn Rhydderch (White Book of Rhydderch), in the tales known as Pedair Cainc y Mabinogi. In the second branch of the manuscript, Branwen, sister of the King of the Brythons, is given by her brother Bendigeidfran to the King of Ireland in an arranged marriage designed to broker peace between the two countries. She is forced to live in a strange land and ordered to work in the kitchens, where she is slapped round the face with a slab of meat each day, her only friend a starling who flies over the sea with messages for her brother. In the third branch, following the wars with the Irish, the King's brother, Manawydan, emigrates to England to find work as a craftsman, but he is too skilled at his job and is forcibly moved on, time and time again, until he finally returns home. He turns to farming and grows three fields of corn, only to wake up each morning to find the ears of his golden corn have

been eaten by a horde of proletarian mice. In the fourth branch, Blodeuwedd, created from flowers by a man to satisfy the needs of his son, undergoes an internal migration, from woman to owl, and is banished to the dark as punishment for having desires and thoughts of her own.

The tale of a woman turned into an owl is not uniquely Welsh. It also occurs in a story from the Turtle Island Liars' Club, told by Hastings Shade, former deputy chief of the Cherokee Nation. Another member of the Liars' Club, Sequoyah Guess, tells a migration story of how the ancestors encountered a group of mound builders in North Carolina and Ohio, discovered they were cannibals, defeated them in a war, and began building mounds themselves. There are mound cities all across Southern Appalachia, built over 2,000 years ago, when Wales and America were only dreams.

The Cherokee also have stories about the fairies, 'yunwi tsunsdi', 'the little people'. The author Robert Conley writes about John Little Bear, a renowned healer, who believed that whenever he couldn't find something he was looking for, it was those 'danged little people' who were always hiding things from him. And while the little people were mischievous, they also looked after anyone lost in the woods. Little Bear left them whisky and honeycomb as a thank you, and in return they gave him a song to call them up when he needed help.

In Wales, a farmer in the hills of central Ceredigion told me that the 'tylwyth teg' had visited his farm all his life, sometimes helping with the chores, sometimes playing tricks, hiding things, but he couldn't say too much in case they never came again. These memories of the little people from Ceredigion and Cherokee are not ancient, they are both twenty-first century.

None of this should be a surprise. Folk tales have always followed people around like faithful old dogs. They migrate across geographical, political, and imaginary boundaries with no need for passports, hidden in the minds of explorers and refugees. The West Virginia folklorist Ruth Ann Musick's extraordinary collection of European folk tales, *Green Hills of Magic*, contains many stories

from southern Appalachia collected from first-, second-, and third-generation settlers who came over to work in the mines in the early 1900s. Some were told by and about Welsh colliers, who were always ready with a joke and a shaggy dog story. These were the folks the Cherokee called 'the Moon-Eyed People', for they were small and pale, lived underground, and could see in the dark.

In the storytelling traditions of both Appalachia and Wales are shared folk tales. The Welsh gypsy fiddler Matthew Wood told many fairy tales of the fantastical adventures of an archetypal cheeky boy called Jack, who fights giants, defeats dragons, and marries princesses. Matthew told his stories in the Romany language, often at gatherings on one of his favourite haunts, Craig yr Aderyn (Bird Rock), near Abergynolwyn.

Appalachian cultural icon Ray Hicks of Beech Mountain was renowned for his Jack Tales, told in liars' competitions on the Blue Ridge in North Carolina. Ray had part-Cherokee ancestry, and both his traditions use the epithet 'liar' to describe a storyteller. The Cherokee say 'Gagoga', 'he or she is lying'. This is not lying as we know it, but the tradition of tall-tale telling, the art of keeping an audience believing you are telling a truth for as long as possible. In Wales, 'Chwedleua' means gossip as well as storytelling, and this mischievous tradition was embodied in the Welsh language tales of Eirwyn Jones Pontshan, who told of his surreptitious affair with a princess on a train in Pencader Tunnel. And there were the Pembrokeshire English tales of Shemi Wâd Abergwaun, who was carried across the ocean by seagulls to Central Park in New York, only to discover they had deceived him and dropped him in Dublin.

There are animal fables, 'crittur' stories, from what the Ohio storyteller Lyn Ford refers to as the Affrilachian tradition. Here are rabbit, bear, fox, possum, skunk, snake and turtle, stories from enslaved people with links to Cherokee and Muscogee that came to me through Uncle Remus. And there are the Welsh animal fables of Cattwg the Wise, about mole, lark, owl, eagle, magpie, cuckoo and a whole host of anthropomorphic animals written by the legendary Iolo Morganwg. Storyteller Phil Okwedy is currently

exploring migration narratives from his own Welsh Nigerian traditions, while in New Zealand, Tony Hopkins is telling stories to explore his identity as a Black Cherokee.

My cousin emigrated to Appalachia in the early 1960s. She was studying Homer at University College London when she met an American civil engineer with a penchant for covered bridges, and they moved to work in the old Welsh settlement city of Morgantown, West Virginia, where they put down roots and raised a family. So I fell in love with the folk cultures of both Appalachia and Wales, two sisters who explore the world together, with baking soda in their backpacks just in case.

Baking soda was a cure-all on both sides of the water. My mother made me drink it when I had belly ache, she spooned it into every cake she baked and rubbed it into cut knees, and boy did it hurt. The granny women of Appalachia swore by it, too, as did the herbalist Clarence 'Catfish' Gray of Jackson County, West Virginia, who ladled it into his potions and tinctures. The grannies called it 'Sodey'.

When I was little, I had a die-cast metal Corgi Batmobile from the outrageously camp *Batman* television series, and it was the coolest car in the world. It was made in the Mettoy factory, which opened in Swansea in 1954, the year that *Under Milk Wood* was published posthumously after Dylan Thomas's death in New York. I grew up thinking Batman was Welsh, and Gotham City was Swansea.

You could also buy cap guns, cowboy hats and Indian headdresses from the toy shops, join the I Spy club – which featured a man in an Indian headdress as its symbol – and there were books about conservation of the Canadian beaver, written by 'Grey Owl', who wore feathers in his hair, but was really Archibald Stansfield Belaney, from Hastings in Sussex.

Amidst all the phoney appropriation, there was Buffy Sainte-Marie, born Canadian Cree and brought up in Massachusetts. She is a singer and pacifist who pre-dated the hippie movement, was blacklisted by radio stations, became an inspiration to Joni Mitchell, created and financed a literacy scheme for native American children, and wrote the song, 'Bury my Heart

at Wounded Knee'. Buffy told a different story, another history, a bitter truth that was never taught at my schools. This was an awakening from innocence.

The stories here tell of the past and present migrations of people between and within Wales and America. There are no ends or beginnings, no comforting morals, no boundary walls, and certainly no happy ever afters. They are snapshots of easily forgotten lives, a photographic album full of yellow-stained sepia images in a chronological jumble all of their own. These are folk histories, stories of people with confused identities, who developed roots in more than one culture. I am not Aniyunwiya or Appalachian or Affrilachian, but their stories are intertwined with the folk history of Wales, tales of grannies and grandchildren with mixed blood. For each of us has our own individual Mabinogi.

Though perhaps it's best not to think about it too much, or the little people won't come again.

And that ain't no lie.

1

Wolf-Girl
Visits Wales

Cherokee elders tell how some of the old ones could change into animals: bears, bison, owls, wolves, coyotes, ravens, jackrabbits, eagles, hawks and frogs. This sounds exciting if you're into Gothic fiction and graphic novels, and you like the idea of shapeshifting superheroes, or enjoy the darkness of fairy tales. But what if you were told these stories as a child, and all your friends heard them, and they happened in the remote place where you lived, and there were noises at night that terrified you, and the old granny who lived nearby told you they were true?

We lived near one of these elders, and one day while me and my six sisters were playing stickball, a dog came up and joined us. It was just a mutt, with one brown ear and one white, and a patch around its eye. Father found us and asked where we'd gotten that dog from, and we said we didn't know, but could we keep it. Father said he would see, maybe if it was still around in the morning.

Next morning the dog had gone, but that evening it returned, and every evening, till Father said he would find out if it belonged to anyone. He asked around, but no one had lost a dog, so we kept it. And each evening we played games, we threw rolled up socks for it to fetch, we put our arms round its neck and tried to wrastle it to the ground, and we hunted jackrabbits for it to eat.

Then the dog got a bit frisky. It bit my hand and drew blood, and when I kicked it off, it chased Father's chickens, and he said if this didn't stop it would have to go. And we knew what he meant. You know. Bang!

Well, us children didn't want to lose our dog. We tried to train it, but it still chased the chickens, so we caught it and took it inside and tied it to our old iron bedstead with bailer twine and told it to hush.

In the night there was a howling and a hollering, and Father came in and the dog said, 'Let me go before the morning.' But Father knew the stories about the elders changing into animals, and he wanted to see who the dog really was, so he left it tied to the bed. In the morning we found an old woman curled up on the floor at the bottom of the bed, and we recognised her as the old granny woman who lived nearby. He released her and off she scurried. A week later, the old granny was dead as a squashed skunk in the middle of the road.

The elders told Father he had a lucky escape. Old Granny was a cannibal who ate the youngest and weakest in the family, and she turned herself into a dog so she could play with the children and work out who to eat next. And that would have been me. I'm the youngest in the family, so if Father hadn't spotted her trick, I wouldn't be here to tell you the story.

Well, after that we upped and left. Father, and all of us seven girls. His grandad was a miner from Romania, and his granny a Welsh seamstress, so that was that, we came to Wales. We settled in a cottage high up in the Black Mountains, and the locals stared at us, 'cos we looked different to them and spoke a language they didn't understand. They had never heard Tsalagi before, and probably had no idea where Appalachia was, and thought we were the fairies. We weren't afraid of them. They were likely more frightened of us, especially as we all had pointy hairy ears. We left them alone, and moved around by night, like cats and owls. And howling was heard coming from the woods.

We kept sheep and goats, rabbits and chickens, and Father made sure the farm buildings were in good repair. The farmers left us alone, though they thought it was odd that we never took our animals to market. Truth was we needed all that meat for ourselves. Word went round our more superstitious neighbours that we were descendants of humans who had bred with wolves. Lycanthropes, that's the word. Soon we were blamed for every sheep that died, every cow that refused to give milk, every crack of a twig in the woods at night, and every nightmare of every child.

After a flock of sheep were found with their throats cut, the air turned black with anger. Father said it was time to move on again.

One night, by the dim light of the crescent moon, my family left, in a single line, carrying all their belongings on their backs, wrapped in shawls and woollen blankets.

The farm became unmanageable and soon fell into disrepair. The corn refused to ripen, the hay crop was poor, and folk believed that the wolfman and his family continued to haunt their old homestead long after it fell into ruins.

The wolf family had fled the country and settled in Cluj in Transylvania, where Father had relatives. They spawned a thousand and one stories and inspired countless writers and artists, not one of whom acknowledged that we had come there from Cherokee via Wales. As they grew, my sisters spread out across Europe, living hidden lives, relying on friends to supply them with haunches of meat, much to the pleasure of the local abattoirs, and the displeasure of parents who feared for their children.

Let me tell you a tale that my Father told me.

• ◆ •

A man was waiting at a Welsh railway station when he fell into conversation with a tall man in a trenchcoat and a trilby hat. The man told the stranger that he had come home to help his father manage the farm. One morning, they found all the sheep with their throats cut. There were wolf tracks in the snow, and as they followed, the prints became human. His father's face turned white as the very snow, and he told his son that this was the work of his own elder brother, the boy's uncle, who was born with pointy ears, slanting green eyes, and forefingers longer than his middle finger. Years ago his brother had left the farm, angry at receiving no inheritance, and now he had returned for revenge. So the farmer told his son to go before he was killed, and here he was, catching the train to leave Wales for America to start a new life, before his pointy-eared uncle caught up with him. And he stared into the stranger's shaded eyes beneath the brim of his hat, and asked if he believed the story. The stranger said yes, of course he believed him, and removed his hat to reveal long pointy ears, slanting green eyes and a forefinger longer than his middle finger. Just like U'tlûñ'ta, Spearfinger, the Cherokee witch who stabbed her sharp forefingers into children and tore out their livers.

• ◆ •

And I ain't gonna tell you what happened next, 'cos it was real messy. You can imagine. But the man never caught the train. And I still have nightmares about meeting Spearfinger.

Back in Breconshire and over the border in Radnorshire, reports of sheep carcasses plagued the local farms. An incomer's pet wolfhound was suspected, along with a black panther that had escaped from a travelling menagerie, and a coven of local witches who were accused of unspeakable pagan rites under cover of darkness. The truth was more obvious, especially if you were brought up in the company of wolves and vampire slayers.

It was me. Me, the youngest of the wolfman's daughters. I came to Wales from the Cherokee Nation, but I didn't flee to Romania

with the rest of my family. I stayed on the farm. I knew all about the stories of how the youngest of seven children could be eaten by a witch dog. But I'm a dark girl, and I argued and fought with my father when he told me we were leaving. I spat on the floorboards and said we had already left one homeland, and I was not going to be chased away a second time by no man. I'd been bitten by that old granny witch when I was little, and I knew what I had become.

After my father and six sisters left, I slept alone in the hay bales in the barn, avoiding the farmhouse for fear the neighbours would come for me. I prowled the hedges for beetles to eat, scavenged leftovers from dustbins, took carcasses from gin traps, stole cooling food from windowsills, and hunted for rabbits. But I couldn't resist the sheep. They were so easy. Trapped by the fences and hedges that were there to protect them, they couldn't escape my sharp teeth. And I smelled the neighbours approaching long before they suspected I was there. They never saw me clinging to the rafters in the barn.

At night, lying in the hay with warm blood in my belly, I told myself the stories Father had told me. This one he called The White Wolf.

• ◆ •

An old man had three sons and a daughter, and he was cruel to them. His wife had died, and he took out his loneliness on his children, screaming at them, beating and abusing them. His daughter knew that something was wrong with her father, and she protected her brothers, wrapping them in warm blankets and covering their ears when the old man came home at night with too much liquor in his blood. And since the death of his wife, people in the town had been found murdered and mutilated, and they feared being out in the dark alone. One night when the old man went out, his daughter took his gun and followed him. Through dark streets she traced his footsteps, until she came to a quiet alleyway full of garbage bins and washing lines. She watched as her father turned into a great white

wolf, and the ghost of a young woman appeared and kissed the old man, and his daughter knew this was her dead mother. The white wolf and the ghost lady prowled the streets, and their daughter followed, silently and stealthily. She watched as they approached a small untidy boy, a guttersnipe, a street urchin, and she saw her parents were about to attack, and she knew enough was enough. She took her father's gun, touched the trigger with her finger, and shot the white wolf through the heart. Her mother vanished, and oh how their daughter cried for her lost parents.

• ◆ •

Time passed, more years than could be lived in a single lifetime. I became wrinkled on the inside but still freckled on the outside. A field full of mutilated sheep was discovered near Pontrhydfendigaid, and dog prints were found nearby. There were more sheep attacks, and sightings of wild cats, or hideous half-creatures with slavering tongues that were believed to be breeding in the area, skulking silently along the hedgerows, remaining largely unseen, until they pounced. The newspapers called it 'The Beast of Bont'. It was time I laid low for a while and found another food supply.

One evening I was prowling along the shelves at the Co-op in Aberystwyth, and was about to slip a leg of frozen lamb inside my parka, when I sensed I was being watched. It wasn't the CCTV. I was so quick they never captured more than a blur. Only once did a security guard see me, but I disappeared before he blinked, and he concluded I was his imagination. But this was different. I could smell someone. Behind me. I turned and came face to face with one of those young men who have the look of a sensitive poet. Curly hair, hooded blue eyes, you know the sort. He knew I was stealing, and I knew he would say nothing. We met eye to eye. He smiled. This was totally awkward.

I took him by the hand and whisked him out of the shop. All the security man saw on his screen was a young man scurrying away on his own, and he made a mental note of face and clothes for next

time. I dragged the young man to an organic vegan cafe where I often passed the days, dreaming of gnawing on the customers' arms, and enjoying their ignorance of a carnivore in their midst. He threw questions at me: where was I from, was I living on the street, why was I shoplifting? And why didn't I eat or drink anything when I was clearly hungry? I cocked my head to one side and asked him about his strange accent. He told me he was from the far North. Pen Llŷn. Aberdaron.

I was leaning towards him now, staring into his eyes. I remembered another of my father's stories, told by his grandfather's friend, Anthony Booth, a Romanian from Cluj, who had emigrated to work in the mines in West Virginia.

•◆•

A young affluent couple called Erich and Lorraine Meštrović lived in a fine house on the outskirts of the city. One night, they threw a party and all was well until a blood-curdling scream shook the air and a young man was found outside lying in a pool of blood by the fishpond. The flesh had been flayed from his body and one arm chewed in two. Everyone agreed it was the attack of a wild animal. Next night Lorraine went out into the garden for some air, and Erich heard her shriek. She had found another dead man and had seen a creature running away, dressed as an old woman. Suspicion fell on an old witch who lived nearby, so the villagers marched to her house, burned it to the ground, and chased her out of town. But there were more killings, one on the Meštrovićs' patio, and now the whole town was consumed with fear. Then one night Erich saw a beast dressed in a young woman's clothes attacking a man. He took his gun and as his finger closed on the trigger, he realised the woman's clothes looked familiar. A shot rang out and there was a howl. He ran to see if the man was still alive, and he found, lying on the ground with a bullet hole in her forehead, Lorraine Meštrović.

•◆•

The young Welshpoetman I had dragged from the supermarket looked as white as a startled jackrabbit in a car headlight. I was leaning right over him, staring wide-eyed, red lips twitching. He must have thought I was a vampire. Blood-suckers were fashionable at the time. There was no end of films, books, graphic novels. I must have looked like a grown-up Eli, from that Scandinavian film, who could only come into a room if she was invited. Though I like to think I look more like the girl who walks home alone at night. She's cool. Much more me. I like Iranian films. No one goes to see them, so I can stretch out in the dark and scratch the seat in front with my fingernails.

He asked me outright. Was I a vampire? I laughed, very convincingly. And I told him he had a vivid imagination, and that of course I wasn't a vampire. How ridiculous would that be? I was a wolf-girl. He choked, a werewolf? I told him to hush, we were in a vegan cafe, and no I wasn't a werewolf, I was a wolf-girl. Werewolves were monstrous creatures that could change into humans, bloodthirsty men, or menstruating women, who would tear you to shreds as soon as smell you. No, I was human, just like him, but with all the emotions and abilities of a wolf. There is no outward transformation, I will always be who I am. I am wolf-girl.

•◆•

Ivan was a good-looking bear of a man, who was engaged to a clever and strong young woman named Tina. She loved him dearly, but Ivan had been wounded in the head during one of the too many wars and he had become like a child. Laughed at by the villagers, he ran away from Tina and hid in the hills, locked inside his own insecurity. A witch found him living in a damp cave, and persuaded him to sell his soul in return for being able to turn himself into a werewolf. On the next full moon three men were found torn to shreds, and so it was, night after night, more and more deaths until the villagers became hysterical and said the werewolf must be killed. Tina decided she would hunt the creature. She loaded

her pistol with silver bullets and set off for the hills. She found the werewolf hiding in the cave, and she raised her gun. It stared at her for a fraction of a second and held out a filthy paw. A flicker of recognition appeared between them, but Tina's finger twitched on the trigger, and before her mind could catch up with her instincts, there was an explosion of fur and the werewolf fell to the ground. She watched as it transformed into Ivan, and now she saw him for the mistreated and misunderstood man that he was. She lay down by his side and held him until the lifeblood flowed from his veins into the dry earth. In the morning they were found entwined in each other's arms, like dog rose and honeysuckle.

• ➤ •

The young Welshpoetman's eyes lit up. This was just too cool, he could write poems, maybe 'cywydd', and be all enigmatic with his friends. 'Yeah, this is my girlfriend, she's a wolf, don't worry, she won't eat you, she's not a werewolf. They all change into animals where she comes from.'

He was going to take this very much in his stride. He was a Pen Llŷn boy, after all. He took out a black moleskin sketchbook and asked if he could draw me. I didn't answer. I listened to the scratching of his pen while he drank a muddy cup of organic coffee with all the sweet things taken out. I ignored the slurping. He asked if I had anywhere to stay tonight, so I went back to his red-doored flat and he invited me in. It was untidy, full of books about poetry and football, and a black cat with pea-green eyes.

I felt safe for the first time in my life. It was a simple existence – it had to be, because he was a poet and therefore couldn't earn a living, and I was a kleptomaniac wolf-girl. Food and money were scarce, but I did my best. He was so gentle and kind, he irritated the hell out of me, but as time passed, his kindness became overwhelming. He soothed me by reading while we huddled in the warmth of the fireside, I held him tightly when the storms rattled the door, and listened to his heartbeat as it slowed, until he prised himself out of my grip so the blood could flow round his body

again. He kissed me on the hand when I sat alone. I liked him.
I had never liked anyone before. It was beyond weird.

Times were hard, there was no money in kindness and words,
and my belly rumbled with hunger. We took to foraging, but
nettle soup, mushroom pies and mint tea did not satisfy me.
I became hollow cheeked and sunken eyed, hunched of shoulder,
shadows beneath my ribs. My old anger returned, flowing through
my veins like poison. I made cuts on my arms just to watch the
blood flow. One day he found stains on the floor and he grabbed
me by the shoulders and asked if it was anything to do with me.
I said yes, it was my period.

I stared at my young man, chewed my black hair, and told him
I needed meat. He emptied his pockets and found only fluff. I met
his gaze and he recoiled from my red eyes. He said he would get a
job, work as a street cleaner or shelf stacker, he would beg on the
streets, anything for the woman he loved. I stroked his cheek and
licked his lips with a scarlet tongue, and told him I would not see
him lower himself. Before he could reply, I was out the door, and
returned later with a side of meat. That evening we ate greedily.
He never asked me where it came from. I wiped the grease from
my lips, kissed him, stroked his black cat who was purring on his
lap, and told him a story.

• ◆ •

A wealthy man had gone bankrupt, so to pay off his debtors he
sold his mansion and bought a sawmill, so he could cut down trees
and sell the timber. He told his society daughter that they were
moving to the woods, and she said, 'What, in these shoes?' and
he looked her in the eye and said she would have to sell off all her
shoes, and her jewels. Well, she was furious with him, and told him
no good would come of this. And she was right. On the first night,
one of his woodsmen was found by the hut next to the sawmill
with his throat cut out. Next day he employed another man and
the same thing happened.

A travelling man and his pet bear knocked on the door and asked for a bed for the night. The mill-owner said he could sleep in the hut by the sawmill, but warned him that two men had been found dead there, and a wild beast might be on the loose. The man stroked his bear and said they weren't afraid, and went to the hut.

The man curled up and was sleeping with his feet on the bear when a long, sleek black cat squeezed through the keyhole and curled up on his face. He couldn't breathe and was almost suffocated before the bear awoke and tore off the left paw of the cat. There was a shriek and blood everywhere. The man picked up the paw, wrapped it in some paper and in the morning told the owner what had happened. He unwrapped the paper but instead of a cat's paw, there was a girl's hand with a ring on the middle finger. The owner turned white, for he recognised the ring as his daughter's.

He went back to the house and found her lying sick in bed with the cover pulled up around her. He asked if he could hold her hand, so she held out her right hand, but he pulled down the cover and the bed was spattered with blood where her left hand had been chewed off. She told her father it was his own fault for making her give up her society ways, and she changed into a three-legged cat and disappeared through the window.

•◆•

Poetman's eyes lit up, and he said he knew that story from back home in North Wales. A conjurer called Huw Llwyd was sleeping at an Inn in Betws-y-Coed owned by two sisters, when two black cats appeared in his bedroom, and one placed its paw in his pocket and pulled out his wallet. He took his sword and cut off the paw, and in the morning found one of the sisters with her hand wrapped in a bandage. He pulled out the cat's paw and it was a human hand.

That night my poetman held me tight, and despite my lack of empathy, I felt something for him. It may well have been love. But how would I know? Each night his wolf-girl brought him meat, sometimes lamb, sometimes chicken, occasionally pork, often

unidentifiable. He became concerned, and asked if I was stealing from the butcher or farmer or the slaughterman? Or were people going missing? Children, even? Oh, God. Would the police come knocking on the door? He begged me to tell him where the meat came from. I became red-eyed and angry, took another bite from a lamb's leg, and the grease spattered onto his face. He explained that he was only concerned in case I was a thief, and I might be locked away, and he couldn't bear that, for he loved me so, and wanted to hide me from prying eyes. I placed my red fingernail to his mouth and scratched him lightly on the chin, drawing a sliver of blood, and I made him promise not to reveal what I was about to show him. And I kissed him gently, and saw the sadness in his eyes.

I took him by the hand and led him through the deep dark wood, past ruined stone cottages and twisted roots, to a lonely spot by a spring that spewed dark water and frog spawn. I stepped out of my clothes, wrapped my arms around his neck, and sniffed him. I licked his face and my nose twitched, and I ran for the woods as wolf-girl. I returned in the blink of a crow's eye with a dead lamb between my jaws, dropped it at his feet like a gundog, and picked the fur from my teeth. I promised him all would be well, providing he stayed with me at all times to ensure no one was hurt.

And so we hunted together, and he watched while I chased down some poor slow creature. The more he watched the more excited he became, and he wrote words about the thoughts of a prey animal in the last moment of its life. Each time I brought larger and larger haunches of meat, and although some were clearly pig or sheep, cow or chicken, others were not. He feared for everyone in the village, and listened to the gossip in the hope of learning whether anyone had gone missing. He washed his hands so thoroughly they became as red as raw meat, and he worried I might eat them.

One autumn day, he was in the woods waiting for me to return, when I came hurtling through the trees with a lamb dangling from my mouth. I dropped the carcass at my man's feet, and hurried past him without pausing, followed by a farmer and his black hunting dogs, red tongues lolling from their mouths. My man shouted,

'Run, run fast, I love you,' and in that moment the blood in my veins froze and I fell to the ground as if shot. He ran to where I was lying on the ground, curled like a foetus, dribbling and drooling, while the hunting dogs circled me, sniffing the blood, and licking me clean with rough tongues.

The farmer caught up with us, and I could feel him staring at my shivering grimy body. He averted his eyes, not knowing where to look. Then he composed himself, raised his gun, and pointed it at my head. My man stood between his whimpering wolf-girl and the barrel of the farmer's gun, and said he would take the bullet for me. The farmer told him to get out of the way, but this silly boy stood his ground.

• ◆ •

Time slowed in an endless fatal heartbeat, and for a moment, I understood my life for the first time. I remembered my dad telling me a story when we were in the Black Mountains, about a witch called Kate who lived in a Flemish-style farmhouse near Southerndown in the Vale of Glamorgan in the 1850s. They called her the Flanders Witch – she could cure and curse, but mainly she looked after the local foxes and hares. The smugglers of Tresilian Cave used to cross her land without asking permission, so she asked them to pay her with a bottle of Jamaican rum, a drop of brandy, a few eggs, and a little cream to mix together to make an eggnog, for medicinal purposes you understand. When they refused, she turned them into wolves, and trained them to bring her chickens alive so she could have eggs for breakfast each day.

Everyone was terrified of Kate, but the stories of her powers did not stop the local huntsmen from riding through her garden and trampling her vegetables in pursuit of one of her foxes. They hadn't shown her the courtesy of asking her permission, so Kate reasoned with them, saying how would they like it if she walked through their gardens and dug up their croquet lawns and killed their pet cats? And anyway, the fox they were chasing was a personal friend

of hers who had every right to borrow the odd chicken, for they had plenty to spare. Really, they should be ashamed of themselves.

But the huntsmen were unrepentant. They sat up there on their horses, looked down their noses at her, and threatened to burn her house to the ground if she stood in the way of the hunt. Well, what could a poor harmless old woman do in the face of such big strong powerful men? Well, this is what she did. She turned herself into a hare and ran out in front of the hunt, exciting the hounds so much they followed her and not the fox. She taunted and tormented those hounds, and led the huntsmen through swamps and bogs, through blackthorn and bramble, until the dogs were covered in mud and slime, and the men's coats were torn by thorns, until the horses refused to go on. And all the while, the fox slipped into the huntsmen's houses and borrowed a couple of cheeses, some bread, and several bottles of wine, and that evening she and Kate had a fine feast at the expense of the men who had tried to hunt the witches of Southerndown.

• ◆ •

Time was still passing but my final heartbeat was far from finished. My eyes were wide, I was breathing heavily and staring wildly into the distance, thinking of my father. The dogs were licking me, and my man was standing over me with the farmer's gun in his face. The farmer spat on the ground and said that now he knew I was a werewolf, he would skin the pair of us alive if I ever stole one of his sheep again. And he lowered his gun.

My man spoke up and said that I was no werewolf, I was a wolf-girl, and he wrapped me in his coat and lifted me to my feet, scooped me in his arms. He told the farmer never to make that mistake again and he carried me home, took me to bed, warmed me in his embrace and filled hot-water bottles for my cold feet. He spent his last few pennies on cat meat, made cuts in his arm and drained his blood into a saucer for me to lap up, he picked up roadkill and searched the woods for dead and dying creatures.

But as time passed I grew weaker and paler and thinner, and I was wasting away. He stared at his hands, and saw the fingers of a poet, not a killer.

He followed the only option left to him, this gentle and kind young man. He took poorly paid jobs as a driver, a postman, a shop assistant, a night worker. He cooked me roasted sweet potatoes and told me it was chicken. I grew stronger, and found a job stocking shelves in the Co-op at night, and it kept me off the streets. He worked hard all his life, so hard that he never again wrote another word of poetry. We looked after the local foxes and hares, and supported the reintroduction of wolves into Wales, only because he knew they would keep me company.

In time his hair turned to snow and he grew wrinkles around his eyes, while I never looked a day older than when I first met him, although I was wrinkled on the inside. We look an odd couple. People think I am his granddaughter, but he has never stopped loving his wolf-girl, and after all this time, I love him.

I think.

2

The Moon-Eyed
People

Once, long ago, in the Moontime, there was a girl, and she was changing. There had been drops of blood. Her mother told her she had reached the age when she should take a husband. But she already knew who she would marry. When twilight came, she walked down to the river, where she had built a house beneath an upturned canoe, and when the moonlight shone into her home she dreamed of making love to the Moon. She watched him, glowing brightly, full and round, and her heart melted. She would be Moon-girl.

Her mother told her that she was being silly and that there were plenty of nice boys in the village and she should choose one of flesh and blood. But she thought all the village boys had feet of clay and faces of acne, and not one shone as brightly as her Moon.

One night, Moon vanished from the sky, hidden behind a cloud, and she worried he had left her and whether he would ever return. As she stared into the water where Moon's reflection had been, a young man appeared, naked as the day and glowing brightly. He gazed on her long black shiny hair in plaits, her deep almond eyes, and her smile like a crescent moon. He told her to close her eyes and he lifted her into the sky, and the wonder of the whole world opened up in front of her.

She found herself on a red sandstone earth, where she saw a small wooden cottage with a red-tiled roof, smoke billowing from the chimney, and redbud growing around the door, one room downstairs, a fire blazing in the hearth, and a bedroom upstairs reached by a rickety wooden staircase that Moon was far too busy to fix. The front yard contained every kind of flower and fern, dog rose and honeysuckle, and every fluttering, crawly thing and creeping, bitey thing, caterpillars and spiders and millipedes. The back yard was a forest of every kind of tree, cedar and rosewood, maple and dogwood, and every bird and animal, coyote and possum, raven and hummingbird. Moon told her that she could care for these creatures, feed and water them, and if they increased and grew, then he may consider taking her for his wife. Meanwhile, she was to sleep in the woods and never enter his house.

Moon-girl bit her tongue.

• ◆ •

On the day Nanyehi was born in the Cherokee town of Chota, Tennessee, in 1738, a white wolf loped across the moon. Her mother was Wolf Clan, and her father from the Delaware, and they nicknamed her Tsistunagiska, 'Wild Rose', for her skin was as soft as rose petals. She played stickball with the other children, tended the shared gardens, and learned how to fire a gun, for she grew up in a wild place and unstable time. People were fighting people, settlers were at war with settlers, skirmishes and feuds were commonplace.

Nanyehi watched her uncle, Attakullakulla. He allowed a group of Moravian missionaries access to his land in exchange for the building of schools. Some accused him of pandering to the Christians, while others believed he was using them to fund a Tsalagi education system. Her uncle walked a tightrope: he balanced people and settlers in either hand, and from him she

learned the route to peace was through smoking a pipe and speaking words. She could do this. Her people's law was overseen by women, and the men listened.

When she was 16, Nanyehi fell in love with a shining warrior called Tsu-la, 'Kingfisher'. All the girls adored him, but she was the one his eyes fell upon. She had long black hair streaming down her back, she was clever and strong, her words poured out like honey, and she knew he would be fearful of her menstrual blood, so she met his gaze, and never once blinked.

She married Tsu-la and they had two children, Ka-Ti and Hiskyteehee. During the Battle of Taliwa with the Muscogee in 1755, Nanyehi was at her husband's side, chewing bullets to make them more deadly, when he was struck down. She picked up his gun and led her people to victory, then wept for Tsu-la, but not for long, for she was now Nanyehi, War Woman. And she knew this gave her the strength to lead her people into peace. She was presented with a black slave who had belonged to a Muscogee warrior she had slain. Nanyehi was 17, and she had already lived a long life.

She was honoured with the title of Ghigau, a title given only to the most beloved of women. As Ghigau, she held a voting seat in the Council of Chiefs, with the power to imprison or free people, so she became a mediator, always pursuing peace rather than war. She was fearless, and never bit her tongue.

•◆•

Moon-girl worked hard by day. She watered the garden and sowed seeds, tended to the animals and built them nesting boxes, and the creatures of the forest multiplied. Soon her work was done, but she hardly saw Moon, he was so busy shining his light at night.

She said, 'Moon, I have finished all my work, yet you go out every night and you work hard, and I am separated from my people. Please, I can come with you. I am strong and clever, I can stand by your side.'

Moon replied, 'Your work is here, and I have much to do and you take too much of my time loving me. But you may enter my house, keep the fire blazing in the hearth, cook food for yourself, clear the cobwebs and the spiders, and I will visit you during the day. But on no account open the drapes that cover the windows.'

She twisted her hair in her fingers and considered telling Moon what he could do with his drapes. She doubted her love, but she looked into the sky and watched him as he shone his light on the world, and she knew if she helped him, the creatures who lived on the red earth would flourish. She lit a fire, watered the garden, fed the bats and owls, and at the end of the night she settled down beneath an old cedar tree and read stories from her book to Moon, while he lit the pages with his moonlight.

From the sky, Moon watched her and saw how she cared for the world, tended the garden, and how hard she worked. Her hair was the very colour of the red earth itself, her lips as red as the fire that blazed in the hearth, and her cheeks pinched as crimson as the redbud that grew around the door. He climbed out of his reflection in the water, full and bright, he took her by the hand, led her up the garden path through the creaking front door, up the rickety wooden staircase that he was far too busy to mend, and onto their old iron bedstead, where the bedsprings squeaked all night long.

Night after night this went on, and sometimes he was thin and bent and weak, and then she took him by the hand, led him up the garden path through the creaking front door, up the rickety wooden staircase that he was too busy to mend, onto their old iron bedstead, and she held him in her arms and kissed him gently until he was bright once again, and the bedsprings remained silent.

One evening she told him he looked cold and pale and that she could warm him. She took some ashes and rubbed his face with her hot hands. That night when Moon rose in the sky, he was covered in craters.

Then one night, she looked up into the night sky and blinked her eyes. Was this her imagination? No. There in the sky, was another Moon.

•◆•

Nanyehi married another man, Bryant Ward, an English trader who lived within the Cherokee Nation. She did not love him, but she took him. He called her Nancy, they had a child, Elizabeth Betsy Ward, and then he vanished. She knew he would. With her daughter by her side, she searched for him, and they found Bryant Ward in South Carolina living with another wife and children. This family were kind to her, but this was not acceptable. This man was incapable of being faithful, and she would always be a second wife through his eyes. She had no feeling in her soul for this bigamist. He had served his usefulness. He had given her what she wished for: a voice in both worlds.

She was Nancy to the settlers, Nanyehi to the people, and Ma'am to the enslaved. As a woman and a warrior, she spoke of an end to war between people. In 1781, at a meeting between settlers and natives, she said: 'You know that women are always looked upon as nothing, but we are your mothers; you are our sons. Our cry is all for peace; let it continue. This peace must last forever. Let your women's sons be ours; let our sons be yours. Let your women hear our words.'

She saved the life of a woman called Mrs Bean, who in gratitude taught her how to domesticate animals and grow corn, and so Nanyehi became the first farmer amongst her people. She learned how to quilt and sew, she made clothes from cotton, and soon there was a division between the women who farmed and the men who hunted. She traded with the British and was given more black slaves to help with the agricultural work. For this, they called her 'civilised'.

Nanyehi was torn between a desire for peace and a need to protect her people's land. In 1780, she informed the untrustworthy soldier and politician John Sevier of an impending attack by the Cherokee, which resulted in him leading his troops into a brutal battle at Boyd's Creek, followed by the capture of Chota and the burning of villages. She also worked with Chief Oconostota, most

beloved man of the Cherokee, who had chosen to fight along-side the British at the beginning of their Revolutionary War, but switched sides to support the European Americans.

John Sevier wrote in a letter in 1810 that Oconostota had told him:

> It is handed down by our forefathers that ... white people, who had formerly inhabited the country, while the Cherokees lived lower down in the country, now called South Carolina, and that a war existed between the two nations for many years. At length the whites proposed to the Indians, that if they would exchange prisoners, and cease hostilities, they would leave the country, and never more return ... I (Sevier) have heard my grandfather and other old people say, that they were a people called Welsh; that they had crossed the great water, and landed near the mouth of Alabama river, and were finally driven to the heads of its waters ... Many years past I happened in company with a Frenchman, who lived with the Cherokees ... He informed me, 'that he had been high up the Missouri, and traded several months with the Welsh tribe; that they spoke much of the Welsh dialect, and although their customs were savage and wild, yet many of them, particularly the females were very fair and white, and frequently told him, they had sprung from a white nation of people; also stated they had yet some small scraps of books remaining among them, but in such tattered and destructive order, that nothing intelligible remained.'

The first known Welsh in America arrived in the 1660s, a group of Baptists lead by John Myles from Swansea. They left the Plymouth Brethren to found their own settlement in Rhode Island, which they called 'Swanzey'. Twenty years later, Pennsylvania was filling with Welsh Baptists and Quakers, and by the 1730s they had made their way downriver to North Carolina, while at the same time the Welsh Tract was established in South Carolina. The Cherokee were already there, with open minds to Christianity and a desire for appeasement in order to avoid wars over land. Many treaties

were agreed to honour native land rights, but all of them were ultimately broken. The British and the Europeans took the land. Missionaries took their souls. Artists and showmen took their likenesses. The army took their lives. Little wonder Nanyehi did not know who were her friends.

The Cherokee were referred to as living in Pumpkintown, a racist comment about skin colour. In return, they called the Welsh 'Moon-Eyed People', not because they were small, white skinned, and the men bearded, but because they lived underground and could see well in the dark. They were miners. They lived by the light of the Moon.

•◆•

Moon-girl could not take her eyes from this bright New Moon that had appeared in the sky next to her Old Moon. Her heart beat like a drum, and as she stared, she heard a voice. It said:

'You are the most beautiful woman I have ever seen.' She turned her face away, blushed as bright as the redbuds that grew round her door, and ran half-stumbling up the gravelly path to the cottage. She closed the door behind her and barred it with her back, and there she stayed for who-knows-how-long, breathing heavily. Moon had told her never to look behind the drapes that covered the windows, but she had to know if she had imagined this second moon.

She pulled back the drapes, and there he was, New Moon, shining more brightly now, and her heart was on fire. She closed the curtains and stayed indoors for the rest of the night, dusting the spiders and polishing the cobwebs, and every few moments gazing out of the window.

That day, all she could think about was New Moon. She couldn't concentrate on her jobs, she fed grass to the trees and watered the rabbits, and as twilight fell she hung a possum on the washing line as if it were a pair of socks. In the evening, she looked up and there he was, New Moon, shimmering brightly now, and she heard the voice again:

'You are the most beautiful woman I have ever seen. I can offer you a new world away from your old Moon. Shall I come down?' This time she did not turn, she flushed as crimson as the redbuds that grew round her door, then she heard herself say, 'Yes.' The sound of her voice startled her. She became aware of a light behind her, and she turned and there, emerging from the woods was a beautiful young man, glowing brightly and as naked as a newborn.

He took her by the hand, kissed her and led her up the gravelly garden path, through the old oak door, up the rickety wooden stairs that Moon was too busy to repair, and onto the iron bedstead, where the bedsprings squeaked all night long. Then he left. At the end of the night Moon climbed down from the sky and said, 'My dear, I have not seen you all night, are you well?' and she hid beneath the quilt.

The next night the same thing happened, one Moon by night and one Moon by day, until two weeks passed. Then Old Moon climbed down from the sky and he was thin and bent and weak, and he said to her, 'My dear, your hair is redder than the sandstone earth, your lips redder than the fire in our hearth, your cheeks pinched redder than the redbuds that grow round our door, your eyes sparkle brighter than the stars. What has done this to you?' And with that she told him about New Moon and waited to hear what he would say. She had never seen him angry before.

He thought quietly for a moment and said, 'My dear, you have never glowed like this. Whatever this New Moon is giving you is something I cannot offer. I will not deprive you of this.' And with that he kissed her gently on the forehead and began to climb back into the sky. Then he paused, turned, and added, 'But if this moon harms one hair on your head, I will hunt him down and pinch out his light, as a finger and thumb would extinguish a candle.' And with that, he continued to climb.

From that day, New Moon cursed Old Moon, and his visits became less regular, the love-making less arousing, until one night Moon-girl looked up into the sky and he was gone. She gazed at her old lover Moon, who was shining brighter than ever, so brightly that he terrified her, and she knew the anger would lead to war.

She was finished with these warring Moons. She left the house and returned to the forest, where she painted her world with seeds and berries, and the trees and plants blossomed under her care. She tended the night animals who multiplied in the moonlight, and fed the day animals who foraged in the sunlight. But she knew the feud between these two Moons would not end well for her red earth.

• ◆ •

Nanyehi, Nancy Ward, spent her life trying to broker peace between warring men, but nothing could protect the Tsalagi women from encroachment on their land. Her people warned her against appeasement, that she would be repaid with endless broken promises. When she was too fragile to attend a peace gathering in 1817, she wrote, 'Your mothers and sisters ask and beg of you not to part with any more of our land. I have great many grandchildren which I wish them to do well on our land.'

When Granny Ward joined her ancestors in the spirit world in 1822, a white swan flew into the air, and her soul was released at last. The girl they nicknamed 'Tsistunagiska', 'Wild Rose', passed back into the red earth.

She once had a vision that showed a great line of people marching west, mothers with babies in arms, fathers with small children on their backs, grandmothers and grandfathers carrying large bundles, white soldiers with guns by their side, and a trail of the weak and sick behind them.

In 1838, Nanyehi's people were forcibly evicted from their land by President Andrew Jackson's Indian Removal Act, and marched along with enslaved people under armed military guard to present-day Oklahoma. 4,000 died of starvation, disease, and cold. Women cried for their children, and their tears left behind a trail of white roses, with seven leaves for the seven clans of the Cherokee, and golden centres to remember the greed for land. The women knew they had created this beauty in the midst of sadness, and now they

had the courage to protect their children who would found a new Cherokee nation in the West.

The Cherokee Rose grows all along 'the trail where they cried', 'nu na hi du na tlo hi lu i'. The rose is known to botanists as Rosa Laevigata, a native of China, Laos, Vietnam, and Taiwan, and was introduced into America in the 1780s. It, too, had been uprooted from its homeland and planted in a strange world.

3

Where the Welsh Came From

L et me introduce myself. I am Siaci, son of Dafydd Ifan, and I work as the gravedigger here in Llangwyryfon, on the little mountain, Mynydd Bach. I am an old, stooped-back crow who takes pleasure in making beds for the dead. This cold clay is an archive of the stories of everybody who sleeps here. You can read the passage of time in the soil. Look. This piece of earth has never been dug before. Whoever is laid here will be buried in virgin ground.

The church is dedicated to a village girl, Ursula, who was sent to Armorica, Brittany, by her father to marry Conan Meriadoc. She took 11,000 virgin handmaidens with her, but they were all beheaded in a battle in Cologne, every one of them.

Now, I have buried them all, rich and poor, old and young, magistrates and criminals, preachers and blasphemers, drunkards and teetotallers, writers and illiterates, fiddlers and harpists, artists and academics, and I can tell you, there wasn't a single virgin amongst them, and they all had heads.

I was born in a stone cottage amidst the bogs and swamps of Mynydd Bach. Can you see us, clinging to the rocks by our fingernails? My father, Dafydd, scraped a living quarrying stone to

build houses and roads, and digging peat to burn in the hearth to keep his children warm in the freezing winters. My grandparents worked the land before us, and my children will work the land after me. It has always been so, and ever will be.

My people have fought landowners for generations for the rights to live on the common lands. Let me tell you how we came here.

•◆•

The King of Persia was a ruthless man who tormented and taxed the nomadic tribes who lived around his palace, and if they complained, they were slaughtered by his soldiers. But these nomads were wild warriors, and one day a wily old chieftain decided enough was enough. He took the eggs of fifty Rohs, large flightless birds who roamed the plains, and ordered fifty men to raise them as battle chargers. The Rohs were strong, with scales on their necks and thick feathers on their bodies, so when bridled and ridden into battle, they were indestructible. They tore the Persian army to pieces.

The king, however, was not a man to be defeated. He ordered a powerful conjurer to cast a spell that turned the Rohs into fairies, an enchantment that was to last for 3,000 years. The Rohs hid beneath the forests and below the water, and soon the tribes had nothing to protect them from persecution.

They returned to lives of torment and taxation, until they were left with little choice but to flee Persia. The fairies went with them as they walked towards the west, living as nomads, robbing and stealing out of desperation, until they came to a peaceful place. Here they built a great walled city and they named it Troy.

One day, they looked over the city walls and saw a large wooden caravan parked outside the main gates. It was gilded with gold, with eight broad wheels and a man's head carved on the front. For three days they watched from the ramparts, until inquisitiveness got the better of them, and on the third day, they opened the gates and hauled the caravan into the city. They were admiring the craftwork when the door of the caravan creaked open and 150

fierce warriors clad in golden armour leapt out. One man blew on a trumpet, more warriors rushed through the open gates, and there was a terrible slaughter.

A handful of the tribe and a few fairies escaped the massacre, and they fled further west, into the Crimea, where the Russians chased them south, towards Spain, then north into France, where they reached the coast and settled once again. They called themselves Breton, and named their land La Bretagne.

Some built ships and sailed across the waters until they landed in a small island. They called themselves Brythons, and named their land Brython.

A few travelled even further west, through high mountains and along rivers overflowing with fish, until they came to a place where sea and sky blended together, and here they settled down. They called themselves Welsh, and named their land Cymru.

All this happened almost 3,000 years ago, so the enchantment that turned the Rohs into fairies will soon be lifted, and the tylwyth teg will return to their true form of scaly-necked, thick-feathered, indestructible battle chargers. So anyone thinking of tormenting and taxing the Welsh would do well to think again.

•◆•

When I was a little boy, the King of Britain was enclosing the commons and selling them off to raise money to replace the warships lost in the wars with Bonaparte. So it was no surprise to the people of Mynydd Bach when one day in 1819, an elegant gentleman from Lincolnshire named Augustus Brackenbury appeared on the mountain, dressed in silks, and announced that he had bought a portion of the mountain from the king and intended to build a castle, as many a man had done before him.

The people stared. We were very good at staring. Particularly us children. And the sheep. Mr Brackenbury considered us rude, but in truth, he was speaking in a language we did not understand. We spoke Cymraeg. Welsh.

Mr Brackenbury built himself a house to live in while he designed his castle. The roof timbers were in place when he awoke one morning to find that his fine house had burned to the ground. I was watching the flames when Mr Brackenbury grabbed me by the ear and asked if I was responsible for this. I stared, for he was speaking in a language I didn't understand. He dragged me to the magistrate and demanded a prosecution. The magistrate explained that the people of the Mynydd did not understand how he could have bought land that was not owned by anyone. Indeed, they believed that the land owned them. So the magistrate fined him two shillings and sixpence for wasting the law's time and let me go free as a bird.

Mr Brackenbury built another house, and the roof timbers were in place when it too burned to the ground. He was furious. He built a third house, and this time he kept watch with a shotgun. As twilight fell, he watched a line of flares flickering down the mountain, each carried by a big strong man. But it wasn't the size and strength of the men that was so frightening, it was that each and every one of them was dressed in a skirt, an apron, a blouse, a shawl, mop caps on their heads, and one or two of them even wore Welsh ladies' hats. Mr Brackenbury raised his gun and pointed it at the ringleader, my father, Dafydd Ifan y Gof.

There was a moment of silence, when birdsong and heartbeats stopped, then Mr Brackenbury lowered his gun, for how ridiculous would it be to shoot a man in a frock? We burned his house to the ground. He had to be dragged from the flames, and his coat buttons were as hot as roasted chestnuts. Mr Brackenbury's face turned scarlet. He put up posters offering huge rewards in exchange for information about the ringleaders, but as they were written in a language the people of the mountain didn't understand, no one claimed the money.

This was war!

Mr Brackenbury went away and returned with stone, timber and watchmen, transported on ships from Scandinavia. He built a road from the sea at Llanrhystud to carry his belongings safely to

Mynydd Bach, and by 1826 he had constructed his castle. It had a turret, crenellated walls, and a moat. The people stared. They were secretly impressed. They were craftsfolk and they recognised fine workmanship.

One day Mr Brackenbury was called away to Aberystwyth on business. The preacher rode around on his pony knocking on doors, and I blew my pibcorn, and they came, from Llangwyryfon, from Llanilar, from Lledrod. There were 1,000 of them they said, all of them dressed in skirts, aprons, blouses, shawls, mop caps on their heads, carrying sledgehammers and pickaxes, and in one night the big boys of Trefenter knocked Mr Brackenbury's castle to the ground. They threw his belongings in the moat and levelled off the ground so you would scarcely have known that a castle had once stood there.

When Mr Brackenbury returned in the morning, he ordered the arrest of every man, woman, and sheep on the mountain. My father and I were captured, and taken to the assizes in Aberteifi. When the police stopped for a drink at Synod Inn, I escaped, but Father was put on trial. However, the proceedings were held in a language he and eleven of the jurors didn't understand, so the magistrate set him free.

The war lasted ten years, from 1819 to 1829, and was known as Rhyfel y Sais Bach, 'The War of the Little Englishman'. No one died, although people were bruised and threatened, carts were thrown into lakes, stones were thrown, and the magistrates were kept busy.

But who won the war? Not Mr Brackenbury, as he left the Mynydd and returned to London, where he dealt in salt and, some said, in slaves. Nor the people who had no land to work and no way to earn a living, so they left in their hundreds. Between 1837 and 1839, seventy-four families left Mynydd Bach, a huge percentage of the population of around 1,500. They chartered sailing ships from Aberaeron to Liverpool, families travelling together, old friends sipping a parting glass, before waiting for days in the port until the schooner was ready to sail to the new world.

The night before they left the Welsh shore, the migrants drank a couple of beers and smoked a few cigarettes in the quayside bars. Then they made a ci-corc, a dog with a cork body and head, and matchsticks for legs, ears, neck, and tail. It accompanied them on the voyage, but didn't necessarily bring good luck. Only if they made it to America alive did the ci-corc become a lucky charm, and then they could pass it on to someone else who needed good fortune.

My old friend, Wil Richards, who lived at Cefn Coch on the road to Lledrod, he needed a ci-corc. He shot a gamekeeper on Edward Vaughan's estate at Trawsgoed, a man called Joseph Butler. He didn't mean to kill him – he was after a few rabbits and there was a scuffle and the gun went off. We all took rabbits from old Vaughan; he had more than he needed, and he'd evicted people from their cottages, treated us like filth. We'd been fighting men like him for generations, for we were radicals in our souls.

It was election night, 1868, and Vaughan was in Aberystwyth at the counting of the votes. He was the sitting Tory MP, and assumed it was his right to win, but for the first time a few working men had the vote and Vaughan lost his seat. The streets were packed with revellers, and armed constables to watch them, so Wil thought no one would be guarding the estate.

When Vaughan returned home that evening and found his gamekeeper dead, he ordered the police to search barns and cowsheds, but there was no sign of Wil. With the help of Dafydd Thomas Joseph, clock maker from Trefenter, and John Jones, grocer of Aberystwyth, Wil had been smuggled out of Ceredigion, over the hills to avoid the road blocks. He was disguised as a woman, though he was tall and gangly, with a stubbly, sticky-out chin, and walked with a limp after bruising his testicle during the fight on the estate. He reached Liverpool and took a ship bound for America, where he was hidden by the settlers who had left Mynydd Bach after the war with Mr Brackenbury. He changed his name to David D. Evans, bought a farm, married his sweetheart Elizabeth Morgan from Bont, gave up the drink, calmed his temper, and

settled in Oak Hill, Ohio, where he stayed for the remainder of his days. He's buried in the chapel graveyard out of town, while Butler the gamekeeper rests in Llanafan in a grave on the other side of the church from where old man Vaughan is sleeping in his vault they call 'Little England'.

I have been to Oak Hill. Amish Mennonite people live there, and park their traps in the centre of town where the old Chesapeake and Ohio railroad track runs down the main street, although the trains stopped years ago. The old chapel is now a Welsh museum with a cut-out red dragon standing outside. There is no mention of Wil Cefn Coch, for although he was a folk hero in Ceredigion, he was a black sheep in Oak Hill.

The Welsh and Amish weren't the first settlers in Ohio, of course. The Cherokee were already there, and they told stories of their own migration. Their ancestors turned towards the sun, and walked until they came upon people who were building mounds, so they settled and built even greater mounds. All was well until one of their leaders was found dead and she was drained of blood. They realised the mound builders were cannibals and sacrificed humans, so there was a great war, and the few remaining mound people married into the Cherokee. There is a Mound City at Chillicothe, a burial site constructed almost 2,000 years ago, bearing silent witness to the lost inhabitants of ancient Appalachia. They were known as the Hopewell People, not that they would have called themselves by that name. Mordecai Hopewell was the man who believed he owned the land when the mounds were excavated in 1891.

• ◆ •

And there we are. I, Siaci Ifan, sexton of Llangwyryfon, have told you these tales, leaning on my shovel in the old churchyard, surrounded by those who did not leave for Ohio and Appalachia. Stone walls and barbed-wire fences have sliced up Mynydd Bach like a cake, and look, they have planted wind turbines in the ruins

of the peat-cutters' cottages. But, you see, I believe the land itself won the war with Mr Brackenbury, for walls and fences and wind turbines will, in time, tumble to the ground.

And now it is my bedtime. I must drink a little whisky from my flask, for medicinal purposes, you understand, and return to my bed in the grave I dug for myself next to my father over 100 years ago, where I have room to wriggle my toes.

Pob hwyl.

4

Lone Man Coyote

A finger followed the lines of sepia ink that marked the division between land and sea on a map of the known world. It traced around the contour thumbprints, it rested on the tops of mountains, it touched the stitches on the patchwork quilt landscape, then swam down a river that flowed like blue blood to the sea. Out there were scaly serpents with spines and whip-tails, giant squid that could squeeze the life out of a person, predatory mermaids who plied sailors with gin and dragged them down into the depths, and black-bearded pirates who would tear you limb from limb and feed your remains to the seagulls. The map was a mirror: reflections stared back through the ripples in the water, and peering over his shoulders were wraiths, dressed in cottons and woollens, eyes bulging, fish-mouths moving silently. They were speaking. Pleading. Beckoning.

He had decided to leave this scarred land torn apart by civil war. He was no soldier. He was the illegitimate son of a dead prince, weary of his half-brothers squabbling over who should rule. He had read Taliesin's description of a magic country beyond the looking glass of the sea, and knew the stories told by the sailors who visited the green fields of enchantment that lay beyond the horizon. He built a ship out of trees from the forests of Eryri, held together with nails made from stag's horn. He resolved to build a new Gwynedd in a new world. He had followers, and they were visionaries and dreamers. Some called them 'Mad dogs'.

He left Rhos-on-Sea in 1170, and there is a plaque in the garden of a rambling old house built on the spot from where he sailed. How long his journey took, how many monsters he met on the way, how many mermaids he drank beer with, how many friends died for his dreams, there is no memory now. But he landed in Utopia, now known as Mobile Bay, Alabama, where there is another plaque to commemorate him. Then, like all good tourists, he took an excursion and followed the Mississippi north to the Missouri and the Ohio Falls, where he built stone houses on the Georgia and North Carolina border, and there is yet another plaque, although this one does not mention him by name. For he had vanished into the wilderness, a wise move for a Welshman who was about to become a legend.

His name was Madog ap Owain Gwynedd, and his story was written by Willem of Flanders in the mid-1200s, although no copies of this man's book survive. Perhaps he was a historian, or a hack journalist, or a novelist who invented the whole fairy tale. 300 years later, the British king decided for his own political machinations that a British man – note Madog was no longer a Welshman – had landed in America before that Spaniard who had butchered so many native people. In 1584 David Powel included the folk tale in his Historie of Cambria, so giving the story an historical truth. After 200 years had passed, there was talk of a tribe of 'Welsh Indians', Nu̜mą́khú̜·ki, the Mandan, descendants of the first Welsh settlers in America. Here were romance and dreams for those who peered westwards from the grey mists of Dyfed towards an idealised past.

Madog was now living in a world of fairy tale and mythology, so who better to enter his story than Edward Williams of Glamorgan. Iolo Morganwg: self-styled 'rattleskull genius', founder of the Gorsedd, writer of medieval manuscripts – albeit in the late 1700s – laudanum addict, folklorist, flautist, collector of folk tales and tunes, political radical, fairtrade shopkeeper, and abolitionist who refused to deal with anyone involved in slavery, including his plantation-owner brothers.

Iolo was an explorer of the mind, who rationalised that if a Welshman really had landed in America back in the twelfth century, he could help forge a strong national identity for the oppressed motherland. So he organised an expedition to search for Madog's mythical native descendants. He recruited a younger and fitter man, John Evans, son of a Methodist preacher from Waunfawr in Gwynedd. Iolo dug deep into his savings and bought John an economy-class ticket on a far from luxurious sailing ship. He landed groggily in Baltimore in 1792 and wrote to Iolo saying it was 'the Madogion (sic) or Death'. Iolo had given him $1.75 and a letter of recommendation to a bookseller in Philadelphia that praised John as a virtuous and honest man, and made it quite clear that he was acting without the consent of any government or authority, or indeed anyone but Iolo himself.

John worked in Philadelphia for a year, then set off across the endless ridges of the Allegheny mountains, over 300 miles, until he came to the Welsh steel and coal town of Pittsburgh, little more than a fort back then, where three mighty rivers meet: the Allegheny, the Ohio, and the Monongahela. As John Evans stood at the confluence, the waters lapped over his boots and presented him with a choice. Which river to follow? Had he followed the Monongahela, his story might have been considerably shorter, for he would have found the Morgans of West Virginia and the moon-eyed Welsh who were living in the mountains of Appalachia.

However, he followed the Ohio south to St Louis, where he was promptly imprisoned by the Spanish rulers on suspicion of being a British spy, intent on discrediting Columbus, which in a sense he was. He negotiated his release in return for promising to map the trail across the Rockies westwards to the Pacific Ocean.

In 1795, now in the employ of the Spanish, John and thirty men set off north along the Missouri, following the trail thought to have been taken by the first settlers. He stayed with the Omaha and spent the winter hunting buffalo on the freezing plains. When spring came, he rode further north, was attacked by the Lakota, and fled back to the safety of the Omaha. Once recovered, he set

off again, until he was over 1,000 miles from St Louis, 5,000 miles from Waunfawr, almost at the Canadian border, and it was here that John Evans found the Nųmą́khų·ki, the Mandan.

He knew this, because a Union Jack was flying over their village, left there by a Canadian fur trader named Rene Jessaume. He tore down the offending flag and hoisted the Spanish colours. He was welcomed by the Mandan and spent the winter studying their speech for linguistic traces of Welsh. At first there was excitement, followed slowly by disillusion. Come spring, Jessaume returned and threatened to kill him, so John Evans left the Mandan forever.

He returned to St Louis and reported to the leaders of the Welsh Society in Philadelphia, 'In respect of the Welsh–Indians, I have only to inform you that I could not meet with such a people; and from intercourse I have had with Indians from latitude 35 to 49, I think you may with safety inform our friends that they have no existence.' He wrote to Iolo, saying there were no 'Welsh Indians'.

He took to drinking in taverns and hostelries, where his wallet was bottomless. One of his companions reported that in fact, he really had found the 'Welsh Indians', and had been paid handsomely by the Spanish Governor of New Orleans to keep his mouth shut in order to protect Columbus's reputation. Sadly, his new-found wealth did little for John Evans, and after his house flooded he became susceptible to local viruses and died in New Orleans aged 29.

But the fairy tale did not end with poor John. In 1804, Welsh-speaking President Thomas Jefferson funded an expedition to explore a trail to the west coast, led by frontiersman and slave-holder William Clark, and Weriwether Lewis, a Virginian politician and soldier of Welsh descent. Their guide was Sacajawea, a young Shoshone woman who spoke many native languages and acted as translator. She had been purchased by a fur trader named Toussaint Charbonneau, and on the route she bore their young son, Baptiste. Sacajawea negotiated a safe passage through the Lakota lands to the Mandan in North Dakota, where she met Rene Jessaume, the fur trader who had chased away John Evans. She guided the

expedition safely through the Rockies to the Pacific, and once again there were whispers of native Welsh people.

In 1832, George Catlin, showman and artist, also visited the Mandan. One of Catlin's paintings showed a Nų́mą́khų́·ki village with roundhouses rather than teepees, while another was of women fishing from boats that he described as tubs they carried on their shoulders to the river, propelled by inserting a paddle into the water in front of her and drawing it towards them. This looked to Welsh eyes suspiciously like a coracle. Tongues wagged even more.

Catlin noted that shortly after his encounter with the Nų́mą́khų́·ki, a steamboat from St Louis brought traders with smallpox that infected the whole nation and killed many people. The survivors joined with the Hidatsa and Arikara, and blood mingled. Their stories survived too, with tantalising tales of Lone Man and themes from Welsh mythology.

•◆•

When the corn was ripe, Lone Man was travelling the world from swamp to swamp, when he saw Raven flying over his head. He sang to Raven, 'Where do I come from? How did I come to be here? Where am I going?'

Raven told him to return to the last swamp he had visited, and he would find answers. When he went back to the swamp, all he found were weeds.

The weed-mother spoke, 'I am your mother. I am just a weed. Boil my children up for food and medicine. Then go into the world and heal your brothers and sisters.'

So Lone Man did as the Weed Mother had said and he walked on until he met a sister, who he offered to heal. She said she didn't need healing, that she could heal him, and they argued over who was the oldest and wisest. They lay down and agreed that the one who stayed there the longest would be the wisest. Time passed and Lone Man looked at his sister and saw she was covered in weeds, for all the world as if she was growing back into the earth, as dead

as the autumn leaves. So he stood up, and then his sister stood up, brushed the weeds from her clothes, shook the flowers from her hair, and said, 'See, I told you I was the wisest.'

They smoked a pipe, and took Mother Weed's herbs and made a world. They took two mud hens from the swamp and threw them in the air and made a woodpecker, who dipped her head into a red flower, and so became the first red-headed woodpecker. They threw more mud into the air and made a night hawk, the first owl, and then they rolled the rest of the mud into balls and rolled them onto the plains and made the buffalo, and so the animals multiplied.

Old Grandmother Frog complained, 'You're making too many animals. You need to be rid of some.'

So they hit Granny Frog with a hot stone and she became the first creature to die. But old Granny was not finished. She came back and told them Death wasn't such a good idea after all, but they said it was too late, Death was here to stay.

Having created this perfect world, Lone Man and his sister had nothing left to do. He became bored. So Weed Mother played a trick on him. She turned him into Old Trickster Coyote, and from that day he never knew where he came from.

Coyote came to a village where everyone was thin, yet there were piles of buffalo meat. The people told him that whenever they hunted, Raven flew overhead. But this was no ordinary raven. It had the head of a bald man and the body of a long-necked bird, and when it squawked 'gi-ba, gi-ba', their meat turned sour. They pleaded with Coyote for help, and Coyote explained they were killing too many buffalo, and that Raven was telling them that if they continued in that way, their world would end. So he called for friend Spider, and they smoked their pipes round a fire and hatched a plan. Spider spun a web across the hole in an old tree where Raven lived, and when the bird emerged, Coyote caught him and threw him into the fire. As he crushed the unburned bones, out flew small white ravens, as white as Branwen in the old Welsh story, and as they flew away, they sang to the people, saying they would only return at the end of the world, or when fewer buffalo were hunted. And the people listened to the song of the birds.

If only lone man John Evans had listened to the birds when he was standing at the confluence of the three rivers in Pittsburgh. If he had understood then that there were no 'Welsh Indians', he might not have followed the Ohio to St Louis, but travelled down the Monongahela River into Appalachia. There he would have found Cherokee and Shawnee with Welsh ancestry, who lived alongside the Moon-Eyed People who had moved onto their land to dig for coal, preach religion, fight and make peace. He would have heard the Welsh language spoken, along with the native Tsalagi and Algonquin, at least until the people were forcibly moved from Appalachia to Oklahoma.

And John Evans would probably have lived a much longer life in the mountain state, where one old granny remarried at 98, although her husband died six months later 'cos he couldn't keep up with her.

5

The Bohemian Consul to Cardiff

In the Huntsman's Rest Inn at Peterstone-super-Ely, near Cardiff, sat a group of humble folk one afternoon, when I chanced to stop there to rest myself by the chimney-side, after a long walk through green lanes. The men were drinking their tankards of ale and smoking their long clay pipes; they were talking about their dogs and horses, the crops, the hard times, and the prospect of bettering themselves by emigration to America. On this latter theme I was able to make myself interesting, and acquaintance was thereupon easily established on a friendly footing. I led the conversation into the domain of folk-lore, and this book is richer in illustration on many a page, in consequence.

Wirt Sikes, 1880

The humble folk who were smoking clay pipes and drinking foaming ale from tankards outside what is now the Sportsman's Rest, saw him coming. He was an elegant man, in his 40s, with a goatee beard and flowing Buffalo Bill hair, dressed in a long black coat, and carrying a cane with a fox-head handle. The stranger greeted them in a cheerful manner, and they worked out pretty quickly that he wasn't from Cardiff. He was American, and he

looked friendly, and therefore there was every chance of a free pint if they sang Ar Lan y Môr or told him about the fairies. They invited him to sit down and he introduced himself as Mr Sikes, and they said they were Dai, Twm, and Wyndham.

'Where you from, bwt?'

'Well, I'm from New York State,' replied Mr Sikes.

'Duw,' muttered Dai.

'New York?' said Twm.

'They have tall buildings there, go right up to the clouds,' said Wyn, 'I would go there myself if I only had the money.'

So Mr Sikes explained that he was from Upstate, but he told them all about New York City, and they all agreed that they would go there if only they had the money. But they barely had enough to buy a beer, and their families would want to come too, and they drained their glasses quickly and waited until Mr Sikes offered to fill them up. Being a polite and generous man with a love of the humble people, Mr Sikes obliged, and bought a freshly squeezed lemonade for himself.

They asked him what his business was in this part of the world and he explained, 'Well, I have come to Cymru to live and work. President Ulysses S. Grant has appointed me as American Consul to Cardiff, so I am engaging people in conversation in order to understand this picturesque and sublime land. I am particularly interested in fairy tales. Do you gentlemen by any chance know of any?'

The men from the Sportsman's eyed each other with that shared knowledge that they were in for an evening of free beer, perhaps even a whisky, maybe a double.

'Wyndham, tell the gentleman a story,' said Dai and Twm together. Wyndham downed his glass, Mr Sikes bought him another, and he began.

• ◆ •

There was an old couple lived on a farm on the road to St Fagans – he was called Rowli Pugh, and she was Cati Jones. They'd never married, but they shared a bed as if they were, and they were known for their bad luck. Cati had a weak chest, Rowli's back ached, their crops withered, the roof leaked, the house was damp, their noses dripped, they had no money and nothing to laugh at, at all. Their fortune was so bad they decided to sell the farm and go to America.

That evening, an Ellyll appeared. It spoke in the darkness and told them to light a candle before they went to bed, and all would be well. Then it kicked up its heels and vanished, and all they saw was a shadowy figure disappearing into the night.

That night Cati placed a candle by the bed and left it alight. In the morning, she woke up to the smell of fresh bread and a blazing fire, tools were cleaned and sharpened, clothes and sheets were washed and starched. Cati left the candle alight every night, and soon their crops were blooming, the cattle were content, the pigs fat. Even their noses stopped dripping.

This went on for three years until one night, while Rowli snored, Cati took it in her head to thank the Ellyll. She stayed awake, and when he appeared, she watched him dancing around the candle. He looked funny, with his long pipe-cleaner arms and legs. Cati giggled, almost imperceptibly, just to herself, but he heard her, and vanished. From that day, Rowli and Cati had to do their own baking and washing and cleaning, but they managed the farm well. They brewed their own beer and opened a fine alehouse at Peterston-super-Ely, so there you are, you see – there was no need to discover America after all, and wouldn't that have saved a whole lot of trouble?

•◆•

Wyndham sat back and sipped his beer, while Dai and Twm nodded in approval and muttered words of agreement. Mr Sikes wondered whether that last remark was aimed at him, but he laughed, for he agreed with these stout-hearted working men, and he disliked many of his own countrymen, particularly his president. Not that he considered himself prejudiced, heaven forfend. But he did disapprove of drunkenness, although he understood that liquor was lifeblood to the labouring man and it would be judicious to buy them another – what did they call it here? – another round. And this time the boys persuaded him to have a pint of Welsh cwrw rather than lemonade, against all his teetotalitarian beliefs.

And they told him tales, all about the flitting of the Pwca of the Trwyn, the knocking of the Coblynau of the Mines, the Bwbach and the Preacher, the story of Guto Bach and the fairy money, and the one about the lady of the Carmarthenshire lake that was in all the books. And they invited him to drink up and they would tell him another one.

After several hours, Mr Sikes wobbled the few miles home to his house in Cardiff, having drunk rather more than he was used to. Well, he wasn't used to any beer, and he remembered he didn't really approve of drinking and certainly not to excess. But he was studying the customs and traditions of the native people, so he had to impress his informants that he was of the same social standing as they were. And anyway, the Welsh were a delight compared with the Germans. Not that he judged people on the country they were born in, perish the thought, but he had once written:

German drunkards are seldom noisy and demonstrative, and for this reason they do not figure so largely in the police-reports as other nationalities do; but they drink like hogs, and bloat most disgustingly, and are generally half-stupefied with the vile swill they swallow in gallons. A sleepy, piggish sot is a less dangerous animal to society than a furious, whiskey-demonized brute, at least.

And he made a mental note not to discuss this in polite society.

Wirt Sikes had already led an interesting and eventful life long before he came to Wales. He was born in Watertown, Jefferson County, New York in 1836, seventh of eleven children, five of whom died young. His father William was a doctor who insisted his son be home-educated following a childhood illness that left him partly deaf. His individual schooling gave him the idea that he could do whatever he wanted, so when he grew, he decided to lead the bohemian life of a writer, radical and social reformer.

At the age of 19, he married Jeanette Annie Wilcox, and within a couple of years he was the father of two children, George and Clara. He felt it imperative to earn a living to keep his family, so he took a job as a typesetter and reporter for the *Utica Morning Herald*. All the while he was writing, and soon he published his first book of stories and poems, *A Book for the Winter-Evening Fireside*. It was favourably received, but words did not feed his family, so in 1862 they moved to Chicago, where he was employed as Inspector of Canals for the state-owned Illinois and Michigan Canal Company.

His ambition was to cultivate a name for himself as a free-thinking radical writer and newspaperman, and there was nothing bohemian about inspecting canals. And he needed to be free, not perpetually worried about money. So he and Jeanette separated, and he moved to New York City, where he found work writing for *Harper's Magazine*, *Scribner's Monthly*, *Appleton's Journal*, *The Youth's Companion*, and *Oliver Optic's Magazine*.

He specialised in social justice and equality, supported women's rights, railed against poverty and poor housing, and preached passionately against the demon drink. In 1869 he wrote 'One Poor Girl: The Story of Thousands', the tale of a girl who leaves the rural idyll of Upstate New York to find herself in the Big Apple, where she falls into drink and prostitution, until she is saved by a dark stranger, who bears more than a striking resemblance to none other than Mr Wirt Sikes himself. He was nothing if not prolific, and used as many as thirty pseudonyms. He was rather fond of 'Burton Saxe', author of the dime novel, *The Black Hunter*.

However, despite his ability to produce an extraordinary amount of work, reviewers weren't particularly kind. *The New York Tribune* wrote that there were grades of literati in the city, with writers such as Thackeray at the top, perhaps, and descending, as the editor expressed it, 'down to Wirt Sikes'. Mark Twain described him as 'a small-salaried minor journalist'.

In 1873 he married the actress, writer and women's rights activist Olive Logan, and they caused a stir with their criticism of President Ulysses S. Grant for doing nothing to improve the housing conditions of the urban poor, having no interest in supporting a social health care system, yet all the while watching on while the rich became richer.

However, Mr Sikes was prolific and loud enough to be heard by those in high places, so President Grant took Wirt's father to one side and asked if anything could be done about the damnable boy. A plan was devised to send him overseas, somewhere small and insignificant that no one had ever heard of, where he couldn't get into any mischief, preferably a long way from America. So he was appointed American Consul to Wales and informed he was being sent to Cardiff.

Mr Sikes knew next to nothing about Wales, wasn't even sure where it was, and like many before him, assumed it was part of England. He spent time deep in research in the Library of Congress, but found only a travel diary and a map. Undaunted, he and Olive started packing, and on 7 June 1876, they arrived in Cardiff Docks. He approached his new job with his usual speed and diligence, and produced a detailed annual report on the future markets for imported American canned food, which was well liked in nineteenth-century Cardiff, although Mr Sikes developed a taste for fresh Welsh lamb, which he declared to be the best in the world. He participated in civic events, laid the foundation stone for the new Cardiff Public Library in 1880, and appeared frequently in the local newspapers discussing trade connections between America and Wales. He spoke out against shipping companies who were doing little to improve the poor

conditions that seamen endured, and soon he was railing against industrial poverty, supporting social care and condemning those who lived only for economic prosperity. The old radical Sikes was back; there was plenty in Cardiff to occupy him, and he was sufficiently far away from Washington that the president could turn a deaf ear.

At least until Mr Sikes's assistant in the American Embassy complained to the US State Department that the consul was not an easy man to work for, being difficult to find when papers required his signature, and prone to taking extended leaves of absence without informing his staff where he was going and leaving no way of contacting him.

Sikes was indulging himself in two of his passions, walking and writing. He was wandering the old Welsh tramping roads like many a visitor to Wales before him, and writing magazine articles about his adventures and observations in the byways of South Wales, particularly along his favourite rivers, the Wye and the Usk. He walked around the wild Welsh coast, visited watering places, and breathed in the sea air. Wirt and Wales went together like socks and boots.

By 1880 his staff knew exactly what the rogue consul had been up to. Only three years after he arrived in Wales, he published a book, *British Goblins: Welsh Folk-lore, Fairy Mythology, Legends and Traditions*. The goblins of the title were anything but British. This was a collection of Welsh folk tales and folklore, gathered in the best of ways, from searching archives and walking the roads chatting with people. Presumably, his publisher Sampson Low had told him that Welsh goblins wouldn't sell enough copies, but they could hear dollars in tales of the British fairy folk.

Here were stories of Old-time Welsh Fairyland, Basilisks and Fire Fiends, Birds of Enchantment, Exorcism by Knife, the Flying Fairies of Bedwellty, the Green Lady of Caerphilly, Cheese and the Didactic Purpose in Welsh Folk-lore, the Cruel Creed of Ignorance regarding Changelings, Prevention of Fairy Kidnapping, and the Theory of Hiding Druids.

Mr Sikes loved to make sense out of chaos. He categorised his goblins. 'So the Bwbach is usually brown, often hairy, and the Coblynau are black or copper-coloured in face as well as dress.' He divided them neatly and with certainty into five classes:

1 The Ellyllon or Elves
2 The Coblynau or mine fairies
3 The Bwbachod or household fairies
4 The Gwragedd Annwn or fairies of the lakes or streams
5 The Gwyllion or mountain fairies.

And he noted the parallels between Welsh folklore and American. So Bonfire night was equivalent to the 4th of July, Welsh ghosts to American spiritualism, and Snowdonia reminded him of Colorado. He loved the castles, the Welsh spirit, and he took too much delight in discussing the longevity and virtuousness of Welsh women, particularly the 'gigantic women of Carmarthenshire'. He described Owain Glyndŵr as 'a medieval Buffalo Bill crossed on a Carolina freebooter'. Despite his radicalism, Wirt Sikes was an old romantic, who lived in an entirely idealised Jenny Jones Wales.

He befriended the Cardiff-based illustrator T.H. Thomas, who provided sketches for many of his books and articles, including his iconic *Rambles and Studies in Old South Wales*. Tom Thomas was way more than an illustrator, he was a geologist, a naturalist, a painter, traveller, explorer, member of the Cambrian Academy for Art, and champion of Welsh artists, whose house was a centre for intellectual meetings.

However, despite his bohemian friends and radical opinions, Mr Sikes never quite managed to leave behind his lifelong campaign against drink, although his views were tempered when it came to Welsh beer, thanks in no small part to the 'humble folk' he encountered while he was walking the land. However, he did have a tendency to stereotype:

> When an Englishman is drunk he is belligerent;
> when a Frenchman is drunk he is amorous;
> when an Italian is drunk he is loquacious;
> when a Scotchman is drunk he is argumentative;
> when a German is drunk he is sleepy;
> when an American is drunk he brags;
> and when a Welshman is drunk he sings.

Sikes passed over to the Goblin world in 1883, aged only 46, and it was hard to believe that he had only lived in Wales for six years, given his prolific writing and research. Olive remarried, to her secretary James O'Neill, and vanished from public life. Until, one day, an old woman dressed in black and carrying an ear trumpet walked into a police station and charged O'Neill, then a watchman on Ellis Island, with drunkenness and non-support. Her old friend, Tennessee Claflin, heard about Olive's destitution and brought her to London, where she was cared for until, suffering from dementia, she died in 1909 in Banstead asylum.

Wirt Sikes left behind one story in *British Goblins* that could easily have been about himself:

Shui Rhys lived near Aberteifi, in a crumbling cottage close to the muddy banks of the river. She was 17, tall and gangly, softly spoken, with skin of ivory, and eyes of dark velvet that could never make contact with another. She tied buttercups and dandelions in her mane of jet-black hair, chased butterflies till they fell from the sky, played with lizards till their tails dropped off, outstared hares 'til they turned into witches, and frequently broke things. She hugged the neighbour's cat so lovingly she suffocated it, though she said 'sorry' several times to its lifeless corpse.

Shui worked as a cowgirl on her mother's farm, for cows were too big for her to break. She walked barefoot to feel the cowpats squelch between her toes, but she was easily distracted. One night she returned home late having forgotten her cows, only to meet her mother's sharp tongue. Shui explained that she had been with

the tylwyth teg, who danced around her in a ring playing tiny harps and fiddles, dressed in red patchwork clothes, the women with shaggy red hair, the men with straggly orange beards, and they spoke a language too beautiful for mere words. Her mother rolled her eyes, but never chided her child, for fear of offending the otherworld. Instead, she stroked Shui's hair, and kissed her gently.

Time passed, and Shui came home late more and more, until one night she never returned. Her mother searched the woods and the streams, and kept watch on the Teir nos-Yspridion, the nights when the veil between this world and the otherworld were at their thinnest. She watched the cwm where the fair folk rode white horses, the lake where a red-haired lady tended her snow white cattle, and the cave where the dark souls lived. A week passed and Shui had not returned.

People searched everywhere for her, police nailed posters to trees, and ponds were dredged. Her mother consulted the two brothers who lived at Y Ferwig who were able to find the lost and confused. They wrote out a charm, and told her to carry it with her, but Shui never returned. There was a rumour she had been seen in Paris, or London, but the locals knew exactly where she was. She had gone to live with the fairies, who had whisked her away to some place of idle or sinful pleasure.

Cardiff, perhaps?

When Buffalo Bill Came to Aberystwyth

In the early hours of 7 May 1904, a black steam train containing twenty carriages hauled by two engines pulled into Aberystwyth railway station. People gathered in the darkness, excitement electrified the air, and rumours spread like a forest fire. A second train arrived, followed by a third. Then, silence. The people on board were fast asleep.

Shortly before dawn, smoke mingled with early morning gull-calls. A man in a tall hat climbed from the train, took out his pocket watch, looked around the expectant crowd, and raised his arm in the air. There was an intake of breath, and when he lowered his arm, every carriage door opened and out poured some 500 people, 180 horses, eighteen bison, and a herd of Texan Longhorns. For this was Buffalo Bill's Wild West Show, here to rob the Wells Fargo Stagecoach, re-enact the Battle of Greasy Grass, and recreate the myth of the Wild West, on the Vicarage Field in the Wild West of Wales.

They were embarking on a new tour of Britain, having spent much of the previous year roller-coasting across Europe. In 6 months 132 shows were planned, beginning in Stoke on 25 April and ending back in Staffordshire on 21 October. Each morning

they arrived in a new town, set up a performance space, presented an afternoon matinee, rolled up the tents, loaded the gear back on the carriages, and slept while the train trundled through the night to the next venue. They had played in Dolgellau the previous afternoon, and travelled down overnight, passing through the stations at Tywyn, Aberdyfi, and Machynlleth, Dyfi Junction, Borth, and Bow Street, all of them shrouded in darkness. Aberystwyth in the morning light felt a long way from home, but they knew they could do this. They were American.

The station emptied rapidly, canvas was stretched across the nearby fields, ropes were tied and knotted, scaffolding erected, and with the silent efficiency of experience, they built an arena that could accommodate 20,000, dressing rooms for the artists, stables for the bronchos and draft horses, and a blacksmith's shop, while the smell of char-grilled steaks filled the air. When the native people set up their teepee village, the whole effect was of a romantic Edward S. Curtis photograph.

Later that morning, a procession poured down Great Darkgate Street. Schools were closed, pavements sardined with people, and children became over-excited. A wild horde of cowboys in tall hats rode down the hill from the clock tower, followed by natives in headdresses, some whooping and hollering, others looking distant and disinterested. There were sharpshooters, gauchos, cavalrymen, Cossacks and Arabians, and the Deadwood Stage pulled by a piebald horse. There was a kerfuffle, the piebald fell to the ground, and the stagecoach shuddered to a halt. As the horse was freed from its harness and collar and helped to its feet, a small piece of painted wood broke off the shaft.

An inquisitive little girl in a violet coat had been quietly watching, holding tightly to her grandfather's hand. But this was too much for her. She wrenched free of the old man's grasp, and wriggled her way through the bodies. She ran towards the stagecoach, a woman screamed in the crowd, a cowboy raised his arm, his hand clutched a pistol, and a horse whinnied and reared. It all happened in slow motion. The girl ducked beneath the splintered shafts close

to the horse's back hooves, snatched the piece of painted wood in her hand, and in the blink of a crow's eye she melted through the crowd. She had a memento to remind her of the day Buffalo Bill came to Aberystwyth.

At two o'clock prompt, the Star Spangled Banner rang out. The cowboy band started to play, and never stopped all through the show. Buffalo Bill Cody appeared from the tented arena in front of a packed crowd, dressed in buckskins and a stetson, and riding a white stallion. The crowd watched intently; farmers rubbed shoulders with university professors, shopkeepers with their families, artists stood next to businessmen, all of them squeezed in like sheep in a pen. They were treated to an exhibition of trick riding, followed by the US military firing artillery, and boy were those cannon loud. There was sharpshooting from Cody's adopted son, Johnny Baker, who had replaced Annie Oakley the year before. There were bareback riders, the pony express, Russian Cossacks, a buffalo hunt, lasso displays worthy of Wonder Woman, an attack on a settler's cabin, the capture of the Deadwood stage with Cody himself holding the reins, and a re-enactment of the battle of Greasy Grass.

Buffalo Bill himself on horseback fired his rifle at glass balls thrown in the air, and he never missed, not once. Johnny Baker shot between his legs while standing on his head, shattering glass balls and plugging holes in playing cards thrown in the air 90ft away. They had stopped shooting live pigeons a few years before. It was messy, and people complained, although they still used live ammunition.

This was just another day to Buffalo Bill Cody. He was an entrepreneur who had once been a frontiersman. By the age of 15 he was riding for the Pony Express, in 1864 he was a scout for General Phil Sheridan, and three years later he became a buffalo hunter for the Kansas Pacific railroad, where he claimed to have shot over 4,000 in two years, hence his nickname.

After the death of General Custer at the battle of Greasy Grass in 1776, Cody hit upon the idea of touring an American variety show that would take the audience into the Wild West without

fear of being shot, robbed, or stampeded by cattle. It would be a
tribute act to frontiersmen, natives, and soldiers, rather like the
Bootleg Beatles, but with gunsmoke instead of guitars.

In 1885, he invited the Lakota chief Thatȟáŋka Íyotake, 'Sitting
Bull', and a group of his warriors to play themselves in a re-enactment of the battle of Greasy Grass in which they had fought. Cody
himself would play Custer, and die a dramatic, drawn-out, and
undeniably romantic death worthy of Lear or Nelson. Sitting Bull
believed this may be a way to present the true nature of his people
to a world that misunderstood and mistreated them. He was
mistaken. During his first appearance, he rode once around the
arena, was jeered and spat on, and cursed the audience beneath his
breath. After four months he quit, and returned to the Standing
Rock Reservation in North and South Dakota.

He had been left with a sense of humiliation, a loss of dignity,
and a feeling that there must be a better way forward for his people
than being gawped at in what was little more than a freak show.
He had heard of a new religion that was inspiring the people in
the south and west, and it was not Christianity. It offered a celebration of life and respected their traditions, re-joined them with
the ancestors, protected the wildlife they shared their lives with,
and returned them to the land that had been taken from them.
This was the Ghost Dance.

One supporter of the Ghost Dance was Sitting Bull's nephew,
Matȟó Wanáȟtake (Kicking Bear). He was born an Oglala Sioux
around 1846, married Woodpecker Woman, daughter of the
Lakota chief, Uŋpȟáŋ Gleška (Spotted Elk), and so became a
chief in the Lakota Nation. He fought alongside Sitting Bull at
Greasy Grass, but he disagreed with his uncle's decision to work
with Cody. In October 1889, Kicking Bear and his fellow Lakota,
Thatȟáŋka Ptéčela (Short Bull), travelled to Nevada to learn the
Ghost Dance from the movement's Paiute leader, Wovoka. Within
a year the dance had spread across the western half of the United
States. Native people were gathering, feeling empowered, and the
government was becoming fearful.

In October 1890, Kicking Bear visited his uncle in South Dakota. Shortly before Christmas, armed police were sent to remove Sitting Bull from the Standing Rock reservation. A shot rang out, and another, and Sitting Bull lay dead. Shortly before New Year, the U.S. Army rode into the nearby Pine Ridge Reservation on Wounded Knee Creek and slaughtered up to 300 Lakota, including their leader, Spotted Elk, whose body was photographed lying frozen in the snow. Hundreds more were injured and arrested in one of the worst recorded mass shootings in American history.

Kicking Bear was in prison in Fort Sheridan, Illinois, when Bill Cody came to visit, and persuaded the authorities to commute his sentence, along with a group of twenty-seven Lakota, in exchange for signing contracts committing them to tour in his Wild West Show.

A few months later, Cody returned to Britain and stayed for over twelve months, and this time he came to Wales – well, to Cardiff. He set up a teepee village in Sophia Gardens, buffalo grazed on the grass in the park, and huge crowds thronged the roads to watch the parade go by. Cody stayed for six days, nearly 130,000 people came to watch, and £10,000 changed hands.

The romantic image of the Wild West that Cody presented that week shatters into shards of broken mirror with the realisation that among the cast were men who had lost loved ones in the massacre at Wounded Knee, Kicking Bear and Short Bull among them. Kicking Bear found this the most humiliating experience of his life, and after a year he returned to his people on the Pine Ridge Reservation.

Wasú Máza, Iron Hail, known as Dewey Beard, worked with Cody for fifteen years. He had killed a soldier at Greasy Grass as a 20-year-old and was shot twice in the back and once in the leg at Wounded Knee, where he watched his mother and brother William die; along with his father Horn Cloud, and wife and baby son, Wet Feet. He became a film actor and native rights activist, and lived at Pine Ridge until he was evicted from his home in 1942, when the department of war annexed it for a bombing range. He was moved to a one-room shack in Rapid City, where he lived until 1955, the last surviving witness of Greasy Grass and Wounded Knee.

In May 1904, Buffalo Bill retuned to Wales. This time he ventured beyond Cardiff, to Aberdare, Bangor, Ebbw Vale, Llanelli, Rhyl, Ruabon, Llandudno, Porthmadoc, Holyhead, Dolgellau, Caernarfon, Oswestry, Builth Wells, Barry Dock, Neath, Pembroke Dock, Carmarthen, and Swansea. He travelled by train, having signed an agreement with Cambrian Railways that they would guarantee the safety of his animals. Cambrian Railways were quite used to carrying animals, as they frequently transported herds of cattle, flocks of sheep, and elephants from travelling menageries.

And so, on the evening of 6 May, they loaded their tents and teepees, horses and buffalo, artillery and stagecoaches, back onto the three black trains at Aberystwyth station, and set off towards Oswestry. Their thoughts must have been elsewhere, for a month earlier a mail train had crashed into the back of the Oregon Express in Chicago after it stopped at a signal in thick fog. Twenty-three Lakota from Pine Lake were in the rear carriage, on their way to join the Wild West Show in Wales. There were terrible injuries, and Chief White Horse and five more died. And the Lakota mourned their dead once more.

•—◆—•

Many memories remain of the day Buffalo Bill came to Aberystwyth. There are three misty photographs that show US artillery being hauled around the arena, and a moustachioed cowboy on horseback with Pen Dinas in the background. Another photo was taken a few days before, of two unnamed Lakota in hospital in Llandudno, with three nurses standing between their beds. An 'Indian' figure stands on the pavement on Terrace Road, chained to Lloyds tobacconists, a reminder of the crude stereotyping of native people. A head-dressed naïve portrait of 'Tatanka Iyotake' is painted on the side of the shooting gallery in the travelling fairground that visits every November. And a piece of broken painted wood rescued from the Deadwood stage was kept in a house in Llanbadarn Fawr. And another memory lies beneath the water.

On the site of the old Vicarage Field where Buffalo Bill pitched his tents, just next to the children's playground in the park, there is a small swamp with coppiced and pollarded alders. Every winter this little piece of land floods, the trees go paddling, dogs splash 'n' sniff, and there are siskin and redpoll, ducks and kingfishers, and once a white egret. It's a memory of the Rheidol flood plain, before the industrial estates, tax office, cheap food shops, car parks, storage depots, concrete, cement and traffic smells. In the summer it is a coiffured municipal lawn, but once a year it is a looking glass, a mirror, a reflection of those who walked this valley before, a glimpse of an otherworld.

Listen.

There are voices still speaking from a forgotten, shared past.

The Cherokee Who Married a Welshman

I n 1964, an American couple arrived at Heathrow. There
didn't appear to be anything special about them. He wore a
neatly cut suit, a straw boater pulled down over his curly grey
hair, while she looked a ringer for Jackie Kennedy. Her husband –
well, ex-husband – hailed a black cab, and asked the driver to take
them to Carno.

'What you say, mate? Camden?'

'Carno.'

'Never heard of it. You sure you don't mean Croydon?'

'Carno. It's in Wales.'

'Ah, you mean Cardiff. It's a long way. It'll cost.'

The man leaned through the cab window, and stared into the
driver's eyes till the air turned cold as ice.

'Listen to me, buddy. I said Carno. It's near Newtown,
Montgomeryshire. I will direct you,' and with that he stuffed a
wad of notes into the cab driver's glove compartment.

'Oh, Carno, yeah. Thought that's what you said. Hop in, you tell
me where to go, and I'll take you there. Happy to be of service, sir.'

The cab driver said no more, other than to remark on the beautiful day, and the green of the countryside, and how his missus
didn't understand him.

I feel I should explain. Let me take you back to the early 1900s in downtown Chicago. A boy stood on a street corner selling newspapers, a straw boater balanced on top of unruly curly hair, with a stare that could freeze a jackrabbit at thirty paces. Work was scarce and times were hard, and hasn't it always been so? He had just been muscled out of his pitch by a bear of a boy who had stolen all his copies of the *Chicago Tribune*. He was filled with venom but refused to show it. That would be ungentlemanly. He remained in control of his emotions.

He was on the streets trying to raise money to support his father's drinking and gambling habits. The family had left Carno in Montgomeryshire a few years before to live in the new world. His father was a farmer who had fallen on hard times, unable to pay the rent to the estate, but the bad fortune had followed him to Chicago. He drank what little cash he earned and argued incessantly with his wife, until the two older kids flew the coop to escape the tension. The responsibility of looking after the family fell on the curly-haired third child, with a gorgon stare and the patience of a cold calculating coyote.

He dropped out of school before he was 13, took to petty theft and hijacked trucks at gunpoint. He was brought before Judge Jack Murray, who was so impressed by the boy's intelligence he persuaded him to study the law while in gaol, and supplied him with books on tort and jurisprudence. The boy studied hard, much to the judge's delight, for he was convinced the lad would make a fine lawyer, maybe a leading barrister.

On his release, the boy began dealing in bootleg liquor, and raised enough money to set up his own business enterprise in a room above a launderette, dispensing legal and financial advice to any hoodlums who called in. Soon he became the unofficial lawyer to the Chicago criminal underworld, so inventing the term, 'money laundering'.

He had many names. John Brunswick, G. Logan, Mr Lincoln, Dave Ostrand, Cy Pope, and John Hall, among more than two dozen listed by the FBI. The press referred to him as the Prince of Crime, or the Camel after his love of camel-hair coats, or the Hump,

a shortened version of his real name, but it was the nicknames
bestowed on him by people who knew him that spoke volumes.
The Brainy Hood, Mr Einstein, and Mr Moneybags. No one could
pronounce his Welsh name, Llewelyn Morris Humphreys, so he
changed it in the time-honoured fashion of so many migrants.
Llewelyn became Lew, but to his wife he would always be 'Curly'.

She was Mary Clementine Brendle, but everyone knew her as
'Clemie'. She was half-Cherokee from Oklahoma, whose ancestors had walked on the Trail of Tears. She was studying music at
university when she met Curly in 1921, while he was on the run
after a jewel heist and shooting in Chicago. He was staying at his
brother Henry's home in Little Axe, Oklahoma, and working as a
door-to-door Victrola phonograph salesman for Henry's music shop.
One day he called at Clemie's house in Pink to demonstrate his
wares. What a charmer. He was slick-talking, and a snappy dresser
who looked like he'd walked out of a catalogue. Oh, and that hair.
When she touched it, it bounced back into shape. And he fell for her
straight away. He called her his 'Indian Princess'. She had beautiful
raven hair and dark eyes, and she could do book-keeping, what you
might call creative accountancy. She had a photographic memory,
and could remember the name of every union man susceptible to
corruption, and recalled every penny that had been paid or stolen.
She didn't need to write anything down. It wasn't long before she
became indispensable.

Curly and Clemie ran away and got married in Dallas, and when
the heat cooled in Chicago, they moved to 7710 Bennett Avenue,
where Curly hung a plaque over the fireplace that read, 'Love thy
crooked neighbor as you love thy crooked self'. After a short time
in jail for tax avoidance, he tried to go straight, and was working
as a short order cook at Messinger's Restaurant on Halsted Street,
when he came to the attention of the Outfit, and was hired as personal driver for their boss, Mr Capone. They were interested in
him because of his speciality in the corruptibility of authority, particularly judges, a skill that came in useful when Mr Capone was
arrested and charged with perjury, vagrancy, and various violations

of federal prohibition laws. Curly used the legal expertise taught to him by Judge Murray to help persuade the court to reduce the charge to tax avoidance. He coined the phrase, 'Vote early and vote often,' organised the Mob takeover of the Chicago labour unions, and helped co-ordinate the St Valentine's Day Massacre, although nothing was ever proved. On Mr Capone's untimely incarceration in Alcatraz and subsequent death following a diagnosis of neuro-syphilis, Curly inherited the title 'Public Enemy Number One'.

He had money, and kept $10,000 in each pocket as loose change in case he needed to pay off anyone corruptible. Clemie suggested he use some of his cash to acquire land around her family in Little Axe, for tax reasons, you understand. They built a crooked house all of their own, with a marble fireplace, a chain-link fence that enclosed 11 acres, and a lookout tower.

They had a daughter named Llewella, after Curly's real name. He built her a crooked playhouse. She loved it. She adored her crooked dad.

> There was a crooked man, and he walked a crooked mile,
> He made a crooked cake which contained a crooked file,
> He bought off a crooked judge and used his crooked nouse,
> And we all lived together in a crooked little house.

Clemie's nephews and nieces called him Uncle Lew. He dressed up as Santa Claus at Christmas and bought presents for all the kids, and filled his pick-up truck with turkeys and puddings and gave it to the underprivileged Cherokee children. He handed out dollars to strangers in the street, and never walked past any beggars or hobos. Skybuck, their gardener, told Curly all about the history and plight of the people. They were all dirt poor, and he had money. It made sense.

The house had a secret entrance, which was used by his Italian-speaking business associates when they came to call. He often went to Italy to visit his other family, you get my meaning? He was mischie-vous, too. He liked to dress up as a cowboy and jump out on people with a six-shooter, and he glued silver dollars to the bottom of their

swimming pool, so when his friends from the Outfit saw the shining coins, they dived in and tried to steal them. Curly just smiled.

When Llewela was 18, her father asked who she would like to take to her graduation ball at South Shore High School in Chicago. She replied, 'Frank Sinatra'. Curly had a lot of friends in the Chicago film industry, whom he was supporting financially, and he could easily pull in a favour. So that evening, Llewella went to the dance with Frankie on her arm, and the boys and girls were green with envy.

Llewella was a talented pianist, and in 1954 Curly paid for her to go to Rome to study, where she fell in love with the already married Italian actor Rossano Brazzi. She came home to Oklahoma and gave birth to their son, George Llewellyn. Clemie helped raise George, while Curly helped Brazzi forge a film career in Hollywood. He starred in *Summertime* with Katharine Hepburn, *The Story of Esther Costello* with Joan Crawford, and he was in *The Italian Job* and *South Pacific*. Curly enjoyed a good film.

Llewella changed her name to Lluela Brady, to feel close to Brazzi, although he never divorced his wife. And she loved her father so much, even when he placed her in a sanatorium in Kansas for a few years. Once at a Senate committee hearing, Senator Estes Kafauver from Tennessee said Llewella was 'nuts', and although Curly was a peaceful man, he had to be restrained from having the senator powdered.

Even the FBI loved Curly, and Clemie never stopped loving him, even after he ran off to Florida with Jeanne Stacy in 1954 and lived under the alias of 'Lewis Hart', a retired Texas oilman. It was three years before she divorced him; she couldn't bear to lose him. The following year he married Jeanne, but he never forgot Clemie. He called her regularly, she logged every phone call (remember, she had total recall) and he visited Llewella and George and his Cherokee friends regularly in Oklahoma. He knew his history, he could tell the Cherokee migration stories, and he knew he wasn't the first Welshman to live with Clemie's people.

There was Evan Jones, Baptist preacher from Breconshire who lived most of his life with the Cherokee, set up a mission, learnt

the language, translated the Bible into Tsalagi, and tried to stop speculators stealing land. So they tried to frame him for the murder of his sister-in-law, Cynthia Cunningham. She worked at the mission, where she died in childbirth, but Jones hushed up her death. He was taken to court in the hope he'd be locked away and the mission land would be sold and developed, but he was acquitted. He bitterly opposed President Jackson's Indian Removal Act, and walked with his son on the Trail of Tears, although when they reached Oklahoma, 'the Cherokee elders ordered him to leave.

The suspicion of murder never went away, although he returned shortly afterwards, stayed for a further thirty-two years, and was posthumously honoured as a member of the Cherokee Nation.

Not everyone approves of outsiders moving in and taking over, but Curly never turned his back on his Cherokee family. He was trying to retire from the Outfit. He wasn't well, he had a heart condition, but he protected them from the FBI, so he was considered too important to lose. But it was killing him. And they didn't know he had unfinished business that didn't involve them.

That's why the Humphreys family embarked on a two-month tour of Europe in 1964. Curly, Clemie, and Llewella. The Welsh head of the Chicago Outfit, his half-Cherokee ex-wife, and his musician daughter. They took a black cab from Heathrow all the way to Carno, visited all Curly's relatives, aunts and uncles, cousins and second cousins, and they were welcomed like royalty. They were fed bara brith and drank a cwrw at the Aleppo. And the family all adored their Uncle Lew. But he was horrified to find that they had fallen on hard times. It was like being back in America in the Depression. They lived in damp stone houses, kept a few animals, had little money, couldn't pay their rents, and were living in fear that the Llandinam estate would be sold and they would be evicted.

The Humphreys left Carno, by black cab of course, and returned home to their families in Oklahoma and Chicago. But a month or so later, their Welsh family discovered that the estate had been purchased by a mysterious American benefactor, and their rents had been paid off.

Curly loved his families. All of them. He died in 1965 of a heart attack, or 'unnatural causes'. Clemie knew it was going to happen. He knew too much. The FBI were hounding him, and he just wanted to live in peace. Death was the only way he could escape, this Welshman who helped create Las Vegas, controlled much of Hollywood, knew of both the election and assassination of his friend Joe Kennedy's son before they happened, was the inspiration for a character in *The Godfather*, and dined with kings the world over. And the Cherokee mourned him. He left stories of the Mobster in their midst, although it was best not to think about where the laundry money came from.

He had many sayings he was fond of, the Welshman who ran the Mob:

'I refuse to answer on the grounds it might incriminate me.'

'The difference between guilt and innocence in any court is who gets to the judge first with the most.'

And:

'Go out of your way to make a friend instead of an enemy.'

8

John Roberts
of the Frolic

An old Romany folk tale tells of a girl named Mara, who was deeply in love with a young man, but he didn't return her affection. She was in the woods, wailing her sorrows to the wind, when she turned and there was the Devil, who offered to give her the man she desired, in return for her family. So the Devil made a box from her father, a bow from her mother, and four strings from her brothers, and gave the fiddle to Mara. She picked up the bow and began to play. Her young man appeared in front of her, dancing like a wild thing, until the Devil carried them both away, leaving the fiddle lying on the ground. And there it stayed until the King of the Romanies walked by, picked up the fiddle, and played music that sang to the birds in gypsy speech, and the birds in gypsy speech replied.

King Abram Wood rode a blood horse and wore a three-cocked hat with a waistcoat embroidered with leaves held together with buttons of half-crowns and shillings. He walked to Wales in the mid-1700s with his fiddle and a few possessions strapped to donkeys. He sired a whole family, Y Teulu, who spoke a Romany language, and lived by the rhythm of nature, the passing of the seasons, and the music of the birds.

One warm still day in 1815, the family were heading towards Ysbyty Ifan near Pentrefoelas, a straggling line of men and women with dogs and horses, and at the back, lagging behind, a girl picking flowers. This was Sarah, granddaughter of Abram Wood.

Sarah stopped to wash her clothes by the river and was singing along with the rattling sounds of the harmonies of the water, when she saw a young man. She snatched up her clothes and walked away, but she had left a blouse in the river, so he retrieved it for her. He spoke in Welsh, and asked if she was from Teulu Abram Wood. She replied in English that she was Sarah Wood, granddaughter of the King of the Gypsies. And who might he be?

He introduced himself as John Lewis Roberts, son of Robert Lewis, the old fairground balladeer, just returned from the Battle of Waterloo, war-weary, and unsure of his future. He had fallen asleep under an oak tree, uncomfortable in the heat in his thick army hair-shirt, and was dreaming of the flutes and drums that echoed through the battlefield like a voice of sanity, when he awoke to the sound of Sarah's singing. He had been raised on his father's ballads, but this was more beautiful than birdsong.

Sarah thought he was one of those cheeky Jacks from her Aunt Ellen's stories, who were always fighting giants, slaying dragons, and marrying princesses. Not her type at all. But they fell to talking, she relaxed in this young man's company, and they agreed to meet in Llanrwst next market day. They spent many days together through that long hot summer. He talked about astronomy and the stars, and how he worked as a corvicer, a shoemaker. Sarah thought he was clever and strong, yet he was a gajo, someone from the other world, unfamiliar with the lore of the gypsies.

So she told her father, William Wood, that she was seeing John, and he said a sheep had more brains than a gajo, and she was to marry her cousin who was pure gypsy blood. But Sarah was not a girl to follow her father's rules if they made no sense. Her own blood flowed through her veins and it warmed her. She knew the Romany had to avoid in-breeding, so she persuaded her father to set John two tasks. He must fight her cousin with bare fists and

the winner would be allowed to ask for her hand. And if he won, he would pay a bride price of two barrels of beer, several sacks of potatoes, and plenty of butter and eggs. Well, William liked the sound of the beer, so the challenge was accepted, and there on the banks of the River Conwy, John won the right to propose.

So the gypsy and the gajo married, and on 24 November 1816, in Llanrhaeadr-yng-Nghinmerch, Sarah bore a son, and they named him John, after his father. He was to become one of the most famous Welsh Romany of all: John Roberts, *Telynor Cymru*, the Harper of Wales.

Times were hard when young John was growing. The family led the travelling life, migrating like the birds, south for the winter, north for the summer, sleeping in barns, tickling trout. Romantic, maybe, but food was scarce, so young John filled his belly with his Aunt Ellen's dark fairy tales, and he learned to play harp like his Uncle Jerry Bach.

'Romanes dika me i bari basimengero.'
('The harp seems gypsy-like to me.')

After the wilful cold winter of 1829, 14-year-old John Roberts strolled into an army barracks in Breconshire and enlisted in the Royal Welsh Fusiliers as a drummer boy. By the time he was 23 he had deserted from the army, been recaptured and court-martialed, placed in solitary confinement, and when released he deserted again. He was living in Breconshire under the protection of a local vicar, and earning a living playing for dances as a gypsy harper. Once, a colonel from his old regiment was in the audience and failed to recognise John.

In 1839, he married his cousin, Eleanor Wood, known as Perpinia, daughter of his uncle, the harper Jerry Bach, and great granddaughter of the King of the Gypsies, Abram Wood. John won a harp in a competition at the Tredegar Eisteddfod in 1842, bought his freedom from the army, and with Perpinia by his side, they took to the road as itinerant harpers, Bory Boshymangero.

By 1850, they had children and settled in a small house on Frolic Street in Newtown, Y Drenewydd. Perpinia worked as a seamstress, while John toured with their eldest daughter, Mary-Ann, a prodigy who matched her father as a harper. However, the travelling life took its toll, as they huddled together in a horse and cart to survive the harsh winters, and she died in her 20s.

Soon there were thirteen great big cubs, and they were all taught instruments by their father. Lloyd and Madoc played English pedal harps; Johnny, Albert and Ernest the Welsh triple harp; James flageolet; Reuben the double base; Charlie violin-cello; and little Willy solo violin. There you have them, the Original Cambrian Minstrels.

Each summer they toured North Wales, Aberystwyth, Machynlleth, Tywyn, Dolgellau, and Corwen, and once performed for Queen Victoria at Palé Hall near Bala. Their instruments travelled in luxury on horse-drawn carts while the boys walked, slept in tents pitched by rivers, fished by day, and played in the evening in return for a hat being passed around. During the winter snows, they stayed in Newtown and performed waltzes on the banks of the frozen River Severn to warm the skaters, while Sundays were spent in the Bear Hotel or busking on the street outside.

And John told stories. He had a big deep voice, and before he began, he covered his eyes and thanked God in Welsh, 'Diolch i Dduw'. In the middle of the story he would say: 'You listening, boy?'

'Yes, my kokko (uncle).'

'Dat's right, my chavo (boy).'

John learned fairy tales from his mother, Sarah, which she had learnt from her cousin Ellen Wood: Black Ellen Ddu, the Witch of Gogerddan, who could curse and cure, bewitch animals, tell fortunes, and make love potions. She was a small handsome woman, with jet-black hair and a mouth full of pearly white teeth, and oh how she broke hearts. She knew 300 fairy tales, many of such a length they could not be told in one night. Sometimes, she stopped in the middle and asked what was the last word she had said, and

if no one knew, she stormed out and told everyone to return the following evening. She always began by saying 'choiya' (boots) and if she received the response 'xolova' (socks), she knew she was amongst travelling people.

John Roberts could tell tales and write in Romany, Welsh and English. The gypsy folklorist, Francis Hindes Groome, wrote to ask where the stories had come from. John replied to say he had learnt them from the Arabian Nights. Groome was flabbergasted, as surely the Romany learned their tales orally? And anyway, he couldn't find them in his copy of the Arabian Nights. John claimed the stories were certainly in his copy, which his father had bought at the fair in Wrexham. John, as a literate man, was learning stories from books as well as family.

John Roberts's stories are not forgotten. His Arabian Nights tales were published by Groome, while the Wood family tales were recorded by John Sampson, a librarian at Liverpool University, who transcribed them from the Romany and published them in the Gypsy Lore Society Journal. 'Goggle-eyes' is the tale of a lazy boy called Jack who sleeps all day in the fireplace yet still marries the princess; in 'The Green Man of No Man's Land', a hope-less gambler called Jack is set five impossible tasks, which are only achieved with the help of the Green Man's daughter; 'The Beautiful Hill' tells of the adventures of Jack and his talking horse; and there is 'Jack and his Cudgel','The Eighteen Rabbits', 'The Bottle of Black Water', 'The Golden Bird' and 'The Fool with the Sheep', all of which star lazy Jack, and finish with the words, 'And I got a big pudding for telling this lie.'

Shortly before John Roberts died in 1894, he accepted an invitation to tour America. However, his sons refused to leave their families and work just to satisfy the old man's whims. Yet Romany people did travel to America, for they were the most skilled migrants of all. And they took with them not only their harps, but also their stories about Jack. When these tales found themselves in the new world, they put down roots and transformed into the Jack tales so popular with Appalachian 'Liars'.

So to finish, here is a rarely heard Welsh Romany Jack tale.
'Choiya'.
'Xolova'.

• ◆ •

A lazy loafer-of-a-lad called Jack needs money, so he goes to a great house where a farmer and his daughter live. The farmer gives him work as a shepherd, and explains that all the shepherds before him have returned with one sheep short. If this happens again, Jack will lose his head.

Next morning, there's Jack, weeping and wailing, worrying about losing his head, when the farmer's daughter tells him to stop crying, and she gives him a basket full of bread and beer for his lunch, and off he goes into the hills with his flock of sheep.

Jack sits underneath a tree, and is dozing the day away while his sheep graze, when a little man comes up and asks for something to eat and drink. Jack tells him to help himself from the basket. He fills his belly, gives Jack a plum as a thank you, and warns him to look out for a dragon who is stealing a sheep each day from the farmer's flock. Jack realises he must slay this dragon, or he will lose his head. But he's a lazy boy, and slaying dragons is hard work.

So Jack returns to the farm with his sheep, and tells the girl about the dragon. She says her father has told her that if he loses any more sheep, she will be fed to the dragon as a sacrifice. Jack tells her not to worry, that he's good at defeating giants, so a dragon should be easy, and he asks her name. She says that's for her to know and him to find out. He says his job is to look after the sheep and keep his head. She says, no, it's to stop her from being eaten. He thinks for a moment, and asks her for a bigger basket of bread and beer. The girl shakes her head.

Next morning, Jack takes his sheep to the field and shares his bread and beer with the little man, and asks him how to stop the dragon. The little man fumbles in his pocket and gives Jack a key, and tells him to go to the stable, unlock the door, and there he will

find a black horse, black clothes and a black sword. He is to give the horse plenty of water to drink, dress in black, and go find the dragon.

So Jack does as he's told: dresses in black, waters the horse, and rides to meet the dragon. When it sees Jack, it shoots fire from its mouth, and just as he is about to be roasted like a potato, the horse throws up all the water and puts out the fire. Jack returns to the farmer, who is delighted his sheep are alive, and Jack keeps his head.

The girl asks Jack if he has got rid of the fiery dragon, and he tells her not to worry, he has a horse full of water to put out the flames, and he asks her name. She says that's for her to know and him to find out. He says his job is to look after the sheep, and keep his head, and he asks for an even bigger basket of the finest multi-grain bread and wheat beer. The girl tells him he is supposed to be a knight in shining armour, but he's nothing but a lazy good-for-nothing.

He takes the basket of food and drink to the little man, who tells him to go back to the stable, but this time to take the white horse and white clothes and white sword and fill the horse with water. He does, and he finds the dragon, which breathes fire, and again the horse pours water all over it.

Jack returns to the castle with all his sheep and his head, and the girl tells him he can't keep pouring water on the dragon – one day it will just eat him uncooked, and eat her for afters. He asks the girl for her name and a huge basket of food. The girl rolls her eyes and tells him he should be ashamed of himself for being such a total loser. And she decides to sort out the mess herself.

At daybreak, she fills a basket with the finest artisan bread and craft beer, and sets off to tackle the dragon. She meets the little man, who eats all the bread and drinks all the beer, gives her the key and tells her to go to the stable, take the red horse and red clothes and red sword, and fill the horse with water till its belly near bursts. So she dresses in red and rides to meet the dragon. When it sees the red knight it turns and breathes fire, and burns the girl's hair, turning it red. The girl is furious; she never wanted to be a redhead, so she takes the red sword and tells the dragon it

should be ashamed of itself, and she will cut its head off if it doesn't stop eating sheep. Then the horse throws up all the water until the dragon is soaked to its scales, and it flies away to America, where it hides in the mountains to dry out and escape having its head cut off by an angry red knight.

Now, Jack has been watching, and asks the red knight who she is. She tells him her name is for her to know and for him to find out, and takes a pair of golden scissors and cuts off a lock of her red hair and gives it to Jack, who returns to the castle. Jack tells the farmer that the dragon will eat his sheep no more, and shows him the lock of red hair.

The farmer is so pleased he throws a great feast to celebrate, and announces that whoever the red hair belongs to will be rewarded with gold, land, and Jack's hand in marriage. Well, word goes around, and every woman from miles around comes to the palace claiming they slew the dragon, but no one's hair matches the red locks. He tries all the servants, until only his daughter is left. She removes her clothes like Superman to reveal her red armour.

Her father offers her gold, land, and Jack's hand in marriage. She stares him in the face, and tells him she has no need for gold or land or a good-for-nothin-lazy-boy who will probably run off with some pretty princess. She is off to America to lead the life of a hobo, and look after the poor Welsh dragons.

Jack asks her name, and she tells him '… it's Jackie.'

And that's how the Jackie Tales came to Appalachia.

And I got an even bigger puddin' for telling this lie.

9

The Legend of Prickett's Fort

In a lonesome house lived a poor old man and a poor old woman. They worked hard but they were paid little money, although they managed to save a few pennies, which the poor old man hid in one of his socks. He was saving up to live in Amerikay, where there would be riches beyond his imagination, and fresh-baked cornbread and mountain honey for tea every day. He gave the sock to his wife and said, 'Keep that for Amerikay.'

One day the old man was out at work when a beggar came to the door. The old woman gave him some bread and butter and asked his name.

'My name is Amerikay,' he replied.

The old woman remembered that the old man was saving a few pennies for Amerikay, so she gave the sock full of money to the beggar. Old Amerikay looked inside the sock and couldn't believe his good fortune, so he thanked the old woman and left before she changed her mind.

When the old man came home, the old woman told him, 'Mr Amerikay was here, so I gave him the money.'

The old man said, 'Amerikay isn't here, it's over there. What do you mean giving all our money to Amerikay?'

And the old woman said, 'Amerikay wasn't over there, he was right here, and you said to keep the money for him.'

'No, Amerikay is over there. And it's an it, not a he.'

'No, he was here.'

'There.'

'Here.'

'It.'

'He.'

'No.'

Well, the old couple argued and argued and went around in circles and tied themselves in knots until they realised they had no savings left. The old man said they wouldn't be able to afford to live in their little house anymore, never mind go to Amerikay and have fresh-baked cornbread and mountain honey every day, so he took the door off its hinges, strapped it to his back, and upped and left. The old woman shook her head, rolled her eyes, and followed her ridiculous old man.

They walked until twilight, when they came to a gnarled oak tree. The old man climbed up and laid the door across two branches, and there they slept, and disturbed the owls with their snoring. In the middle of the night they were awoken by the sound of footsteps and chattering.

They looked down and there were three bad men, all with big black beards. They watched as the men lit a fire, made some soup in a pan, and ate greedily. At the end of the meal, the biggest and baddest black-bearded man took out some money and counted it out, gave a little to the others and kept most for himself.

Each man demanded more, and soon they began to argue.

The bearded man said, 'You will only have more if the Devil takes me.'

The old man in the tree concluded that these big, bad, black-bearded men were robbers, thieves, possibly murderers, so he climbed onto the branch and dropped the door down on top of the fire with a crash, covering all the robbers in soot and ashes.

Then he spoke in a deep growl, 'You big, bad, black-bearded men have summoned the Devil. Behold. I have come.'

Well, the bad men were terrified and ran away, leaving a trampled trail through the flowers and all the money falling like snow in the air behind them. The poor old man and the poor old woman climbed down from the tree, picked up the treasure, caught a schooner bound for Liverpool, and booked tickets on the next steamer for Amerikay, where they would dine on fresh-baked cornbread and mountain honey every day for the rest of their lives.

And there they live now, if they are still alive.

•◆•

Morgan Morgan o Morganwg, born somewhere in Glamorganshire on 1 November 1688, perhaps in the Rhymney Valley, also decided to emigrate. Perhaps he was a Catholic or a Quaker avoiding persecution, or a revolutionary fleeing for his life, or maybe he had a dalliance with a butcher's daughter whose father was chasing him with a meat cleaver. Or maybe not. Little is known about his early life in Wales.

He was 24 when he arrived in Delaware. He settled in Christiana, where he worked as a tailor and merchant, setting up trade agreements between British and American Guilds. He married Catherine Garretson, who gave birth to the first of their nine children. Soon, Morgan was a magistrate, executor to the will of the Lieutenant Governor of Pennsylvania, and a man to reckon with.

Around 1730, the spirit of exploration enticed him westwards over the ridges of the Allegheny Mountains. He arrived in Bunker Hill in Berkeley County, where he built a log cabin for his family, founded an Anglican church, and joined the local militia as a colonel. He believed he was the first white man in what was to become West Virginia, claiming there was not another between him and the Pacific coast.

However, Colonel Morgan's footprints were not the first in the west of Virginia. This was a wilderness of thick forest, where settlers and natives were leading reclusive lives, shrouded by trees and hidden from prying eyes. Welsh miners, the Moon-Eyed people, had walked here from Pennsylvania in the 1600s attracted by the vast coal reserves. Missionaries were preaching Christianity to the Cherokee and Shawnee and Delaware, who had hunted and foraged these mountains for generations, and the Monongahela People had built mounds throughout this land 2,000 years before, just like the Hopewell People over the river in Ohio.

At least two of Colonel Morgan's children, Zackquill and David, continued their father's explorations long after he died in 1766. They extended the boundaries of their world further westwards, until they came to the Monongahela River, where they claimed 'tomahawk rights' by marking a few trees with their initials near the head of a spring and building a dwelling. This was an American version of the Tŷ Unnos in Wales, where anyone could claim land by erecting a temporary dwelling overnight, and providing smoke was pouring from a chimney by sunrise, they owned all the land within a stone's throw. Despite the dubious legality, tomahawk rights were recognised, like a spit and a handshake, much to the dismay of those who already had homes there.

Where Decker's Creek flowed into the Monongahela, Zack Morgan built a fort and founded a settlement he named Morgantown, where he raised his children, Levi, Morgan, James, Uriah, Horatio, Zadock, Zackquill Jr, Drusilla, Rachel, Hannah, and Sarah. No one is sure when Zack built the first courthouse, but the first tavern opened in 1783, and as everyone in Wales knows, a village only exists when it has a school, a shop and a pub.

David Morgan, Zack's elder brother and Morgan Morgan's second son, was a bear of a man, 6ft 1in, powerfully built, with jet-black hair that never went white, and black eyes that pierced into your soul. He had a sword scar on his left cheek and was nicknamed 'the West Virginia Daniel Boone', for they were related after David's cousin, Sarah, married Boone's father, Squire. And he

was a comrade of George Washington. Together, they surveyed the south-west of the state for the Governor of Virginia, and along the border between Pennsylvania and Maryland below the Mason–Dixon line, part of which would later become West Virginia.

In 1771 David Morgan moved with his family a few miles downriver from brother Zack's Morgantown, to Prickett's Fort, a busy settlement of 1,000 people: blacksmiths, weavers, and miners. It was not a military fort. Around eighty families who lived nearby used it as shelter, but despite rumours of native hunters in the area, it never came under attack.

During the Revolutionary War, the Morgan family fought with the American–European Army against the British, but David Morgan was battle weary. He was approaching 60, his bones ached, and he was more interested in doting on his grandchildren. He had lost two fingers in a fight, and this is the story of how he lost those fingers.

One day in 1779, a boat was seen floating down the Monongahela River, with bullet holes and arrows in the sides. Natives were suspected, and fear of attack spread like an epidemic. That night, David Morgan dreamed his two grandchildren David and Sarah had been scalped. He woke up, shaken, but realised it was only a dream. He went back to sleep and had the same dream. Now he was in a sweat, he pulled on his trousers, took his rifle, and ran down to the river.

He rowed his boat over the Mon to his plantation, where he knew his grandchildren would be tending their vegetable garden. He found them alive and well, but he noticed out of the corner of his eye, two figures moving through the pine trees. He calmly told David and Sarah to take his boat, return to the fort, and tell the people to come fetch him. As the children rowed over the wide river, they turned and saw two men, two natives, emerge from the woods, and their grandfather hidden behind a tree. A gunshot rang out, the birds took to the air, and one native crumpled to the ground. The other ran towards David Morgan, who took refuge behind another pine tree while he fumbled with the firelock on his

empty rifle. Just as he loaded the shot, the native threw a tomahawk that struck the firelock and severed David Morgan's little
finger and cut his third finger to the bone. They wrestled, and
Morgan put the man down, but found himself overturned, with
the native upon him, feeling for his knife and yelling. Morgan bit
one of the man's fingers fast between his teeth and chewed. As the
native got hold of his knife, Morgan bit harder. Now they were
both on their feet, and while the native tried to pull away, Morgan
took the knife and turned it into the man's side. It hit a bone, but
he stabbed again with the point upwards, leaving the knife buried
deep in the belly.

David Morgan, bleeding from his severed fingers, ran as fast as
an old man could run and met the boat that had sailed over from
the fort. The men saw the dead native, then followed a trail of blood
into the woods and there they found the injured man hidden behind
a fallen tree, where he had picked the knife out of his body and had
bound up the wound with his apron. He held out his hand to them.

'How do do brother, how do do, brother?' for he knew they
were his brothers. But they took his tomahawk and scalped him,
because the authorities paid handsomely for native hair. And they
skinned them both, and made drum heads and powder pouches
out of them.

And so this story is told.

After the death of another native a few years later at the hands
of David Morgan's son, Levi, a group of people gathered on top
of the mountain overlooking the river and the fort. They stood
quietly, listening to the song of a spirit drifting across the water
like the voice of a bird. A raven flew overhead. It sang to the sky,
the earth, and the underworld, and told the last people to return to
the land they had come from. They finished their song, and stood
long, weary and alone, then turned away from the river, vanished
into the forest, and came no more to the Monongahela.

There is a reproduction of the old wooden Prickett's Fort in the
state park near Fairmont, where living history re-enactors spin
wool, demonstrate flintlock rifles, and cook cornbread in a dutch

oven over hot coals. Each year there is a Native American weekend in memory of the Shawnee, Cherokee, and Delaware people who lived and hunted the land, and a native bark hut has been built in the nearby woods.

But there is no memory of the man David Morgan fought that day in 1779. His name was never recorded, although the men who killed him may well have been his brothers. Maybe he had a Welsh name. Perhaps he was one of the Moon-Eyed People.

10

Ghosts of the Osage Mine

'You listenin', girls? Let me tell you a little lie. My father started work in the coal mines in Wales before he moved to Grant Town in West Virginia. When I was old enough, I went down the pit, too. My best buddy there was a Russian called Big John. He was a great bear of a man who loved to talk while he worked. He always called me 'Friend' and I called him 'Comrade'. We were a team, both as big as each other, Big John and Big Max. John planted the charges and I wired the plunger. One day there was an explosion. I ran round the corner and found Big John lying on the ground with his head blown clean off by a stick of dynamite he was setting. I was shocked, and I mourned my friend, and often heard his voice when I was going down in the cage. One day I looked round and there he was, Big John standing next to me in the cage with his head tucked under his arm. The head spoke as he always had done. I closed my eyes and when the cage hit the bottom, John had vanished. I swear this is true, and I tell you no lie, y'hear?'

Josie and Minnie looked open mouthed at Big Max as he finished his tale, took a puff on his cigarette, and nodded his head. They were sitting on the porch outside Max's old company house

in Osage, near Morgantown, West Virginia. A big black coal train trundled down the main street in front of them, 100 trucks in tow. The girls screamed, but the train was so loud they couldn't hear their own voices.

When the last truck passed by, Josie said uncertainly, 'That ain't true, Max. A head can't speak without a body. You're messin' with us.'

'Yeah, that's a whopper of a lie,' shouted Minnie. Minnie often shouted.

Max grinned. 'I told you it was a lie. But it's as true as I'm sittin' here tellin' you the tale.'

'They got a Big-foot in Grant Town,' said Josie, 'The Grant Town Goon.'

'I saw him, and he was big and hairy,' said Max, 'with bright beaming eyes.'

'You saw the Goon?' screamed Minnie.

'Sure as I'm seeing you now,' said Max.

'Tell us another tale,' said the girls together.

'Well, this is a real scary story, you ready for it?' said Max.

The girls shouted, 'Yes!'

'Well now,' began Max, 'This tale was told to me by two Welsh miners who came to work at the Comstock Lode in Nevada. They moved to Mount Davidson in 1859 after silver had been discovered by two gold prospectors, Ethan Allen Grosh and Hosea Ballou Grosh. They placed Henry T.P. Comstock in charge, and that's how it became known as the Comstock Lode, and it sparked off a silver rush that matched the California gold rush.'

'Now, these two Welsh boys were a couple of old tricksters. No one believed a word they said, but everyone loved a tall tale and a belly laugh. One evening, the Welsh boys were working a late shift down the Baltimore shaft, when they heard the sound of hammers and voices. They didn't recognise the voices, so thought they must be new employees, which meant the boys could play a trick. They followed the sound till they came to a shaft lit by a single flickering lantern, and they couldn't believe what they saw. Two hammers

were striking a rusty old rotating drill, but the hands that clasped the hammers had no bodies attached. Yet they could hear voices. Someone speakin'. The Welsh boys ran, climbed out of the shaft, gasped for breath, and told their buddies about the hammers, the voices, and the hands without bodies. Everyone thought they were jokin', so they grabbed Old Ned, a trustworthy old Cornishman, and dragged him down to the seam. The hands were still hammering the drill, the voices were still talkin' and there were no bodies to be seen.

'It's a pwca,' said Old Ned. 'Run!' and they were out of that mine as fast as their legs could carry them. After that, the Welsh boys didn't play as many tricks as they used to.'

Josie and Minnie stared boggle-eyed.

'What's a pwca?' asked Josie.

'It's a kind of spirit, a goblin, real mischievous, it knocks on the walls and warns of explosions or floods. Came here from Wales. You don't cross a pwca.'

'Yeah, but those pwcas was in Nevada, near Wales, we don't have no ghosts here,' insisted Josie.

'And the headless head was with the Goon in Grant Town,' screamed Minnie.

'Well, matter o' fact, girls, we do have ghosts here in Osage,' said Max, scratching his chin.

'Tell us another ghost story,' said Josie.

'Not one about zombies with no bodies or hands or heads, though,' Minnie added.

'They weren't zombies. They were pwcas,' Josie corrected Minnie, matter-of-factly.

'It's still gross,' insisted Minnie.

'Well,' said Max, 'I can tell you about plenty of ghosts right here in Osage. A man called Robinet died in a fire but they never found his body. Haunted all the derelict shafts. So did the ghosts of three men who caught the Black Dam. Carbon monoxide poisoning. One had been overcome and the others went to rescue him and they died, too. Found in a heap, they were. Haunted the shafts ever since. I seen a ghost myself, right here in Osage. My brother,

younger than me, he was killed in the explosion at Number Three Mine, along with another fifty-five men. I seen him every night in my dreams. I seen dead men walking. And a woman. A very important woman. She walked right down the main street here, past the railhead.'

The girls were completely hooked now. They stared at Big Max.

'And this tale I'm gonna tell you is the scariest tale of all. And it's as true as we're all sittin' here on this porch. You ready for it?'

'How scary is it?' asked Josie.

'It's as scary as a copperhead,' said Max.

'Ain't nothing as scary as a copperhead,' said Minnie.

'Well, you listen now. Here we are in Osage. Scott's Run. Hometown. On the other side of the Mon River is Morgantown. We don't care what colour skin we have here, we look after each other's backs. You think about it, Miss Josie, you got white skin, but back in the old days, over the river in Morgantown, they wouldn't like you speakin' to me and Miss Minnie.'

'You're kiddin' me,' said Minnie, 'me and Josie are best friends, always have been, and we'll be sisters till the end of time.' Minnie gave Josie a kiss.

'Well, that's 'cos you're good girls, but let me tell you, back in 1933 a lady called Ms Lorena Hickok came here to Osage. She was inspecting the Appalachian coalfields, and she cared about us. She wrote to the wife of the president, Ms Eleanor Roosevelt, that we had housing 'most Americans would not have considered fit for pigs'.

'And you know, she was right. The miners back then were paid in scrip, company money that could only be cashed at the company stores. If wages rose, so did prices in the store. They lived in company houses, just like this one. Grandfather of a friend o' mine told me when he joined the union he was informed by the company that he and his family would lose their jobs and would have to leave the town. And worst of all, if a man quit the mine, but his wife wanted to stay, she'd have to take another miner for a husband, or leave. Can you imagine your momma being given to another man?'

'Eeeuuuw!'

'People died all the time. One woman was buried here with a bell, and they sat her child by the grave to listen for ringing in case she was still alive. They heard the bell and dug her out. Ghosts weren't always dead back then.

'There was a big fight on Blair Mountain in 1921 over the need for union representation. Some 10,000 miners gathered near Charleston, many of them migrants from Italy, Eastern Europe, Wales, Scotland, Ireland: men who spoke different languages, but with a common cause. Men like me. Our uniform was blue dungarees with red bandanas around our necks, and so we called ourselves 'rednecks'. There was four days of fighting between us rednecks and the federal army. The government in Washington called in the air force to drop bombs on our trenches, the only time in American history that the federal government ordered air assaults on their own people. The unions to this day have never released the numbers or names of those who died. The museums and governments write the history, not us. We don't write it. We tell it.

'One day in August 1933, I was sitting on the swing on our front porch with my sister, swinging our legs in the air, just like we're doing now, when all of a sudden, all these fancy men walked up with this one elegant lady who was dressed in a suit and a wide-brimmed hat worn at an angle. She climbed the steps up to the porch and shook my dad's hand, and they went inside, just the two of them, no one else. After a while, they came out, shook hands, and I watched her go. My dad looked at me and said that was one fine lady. That was Ms Eleanor Roosevelt herself. Not long after, she set up the New Deal and built a new town at Arthurdale to house the poor miners. We were all supposed to go there, but the good folks of Reedsville, next to Mr Arthur's land, voted to have no one who wasn't born in Amerikay move there, so my family had to stay in Osage. Yours too, Ms Minnie.'

'What about me,' asked Josie, 'Why am I here?'

'Your grandparents weren't born here, either. Your daddy came from Wales, like mine. Didn't matter that you were white.

You were born on the wrong side o' the water. All seems crazy to me. After we came out of the mine, we were all black. And look here,' said Max, pulling out his wallet and removing a photograph barely stuck together with fading yellow sellotape. It showed a young black woman standing hands on hips, behind a table full of cake. 'This here is my momma. She's wearing her best dress, cut from a flour sack. This was taken by Mr Walker Evans, who was brought here by Mrs Roosevelt to document the miners' lives.'

'Where are you, Max?'

'I'm helping Mr Evans. I was holding his tripod. That was a very important job. Only I could do it. Mr Evans said so, and he gave me a dollar for being so helpful to him.'

Max took another photo from his pocket. 'Here, see this, Ms Minnie?'

'That's your house. Right here.'

'Before that, it was my grandma's. See, Mr Evans took this photograph back in 1935. My grandma and my momma lived here back then, my dad was gone, but my granny, she persuaded the company to let them stay 'cos I'd be working underground instead o' my dad. This is a company house, see. My momma and granny lived here for years till they went to join their God.'

'How old are you, Max?'

'Well, some days I feel 60, and some days 90.'

'Are you from Welsh, Max?'

'My name's Max Jones. Got the name Jones from my dad. He told me it was Welsh. From Wales. I never been there. It's over the seas somewhere, next to Scotland. Wales and Scotland, they're friends, just like you girls.'

'My dad told me he was given the name Jones by the school or the immigration authorities 'cos they couldn't pronounce his real name. But I reckon he got it from his grandaddy a long time before that, maybe from a plantation owner. There are folks in Morgantown right now who speak the Welsh language, which ain't nothing like English. But it's only spoken by the old ones. It'll be gone soon. It don't matter now. We all eat the same squash

soup, drink from the same bottle o' moonshine, and gamble with the same dollars. We're all Osage folk. Americans. We breathe the same air here.'

There was a shout from down the street, and the sound of a spoon clattering against a pan. Josie and Minnie screamed and in the blink of an eye, they were running down the street, whooping like coyotes, and shouting, 'Thank you, Max.'

'You run along now,' Max spoke quietly to no one, 'a full belly is preferred to an old man's stories. And I never told 'em about the fight against mountaintop removal, or the uranium workers in Oak Ridge who helped make the first atomic weapon, or the worst mine disaster in American history at Monongah, West Virginia, 360 dead, though it was nearer 500 'cos they didn't count the children. Now, the pits look as if the miners left on a Friday and never came back. Morgantown has sprawled into Osage, like a big fish swallowin' a little 'un. There is a Walmart on the hill up there, although even the malls are closing. But we got somethin' here like nothing else. We got music from all over the world, not just Old Timey and Bluegrass. We got Ellie Mannette, moved here back in the 1960s to set up a Trinidadian steel drum-making workshop, and it's still here, next door to Al Anderson, cobbler and "Sole" singer.

'An' let me tell you, we all came here 'cos of a giant. Yes, that's what I said, a giant. My dad, he told me this. Josie and Minnie are gone to fill their bellies, so I'll tell you the story. You listenin'?

'This giant lived in a place called Gilfach Bargoed in Wales, a mythical land folks call Cymru. This giant carried a huge club with a snake coiled around it, and his breath smelled like a skunk because he ate anyone who came near him and never brushed his teeth. One lad, whose mother and father had been eaten by the giant, decided something had to be done. He was a wild boy who spoke the language of the birds, so he asked the advice of a wise old owl who lived in an oak tree at Pencoed Fawr, Bedwellty.

'The owl hatched a cunning plan, for she knew that the giant was courting a witch beneath an apple tree, so she called on all the birds of Rhymney to build a bow and arrow, and they hid in the

apple tree and waited. That night, the giant came looking for his lover, the witch. The birds took aim and fired the arrow and shot that old giant stone dead. When the witch found her lover with an arrow through his heart, she cursed the apple tree for helping the birds, and the fruit of all wild crab apples has been sour ever since.

'She buried the giant beneath the tree and as time passed, his body turned to black crystal, and spread through the ground. The people dug it up, took it home, found it burned well, and they called it "Coal".

'See, none of us would have been here in Osage but for that old Giant of the Rhymney Valley fallin' in love with a witch. Old Lou came here from Greece, though he was named by the immigration authorities 'cos they couldn't pro-nounce Lukakis. Mike came from Germany with his mom and dad back in the 1930s 'cos they were Jewish. And Josie's family were refugees from Wales who came here to work in the mines. And me, God only knows how on earth I got here.

'And none of this is no lie.'

Brer Bear and the Carmarthenshire Muck Heap

There are three wooden slave houses at Stagville in North Carolina, on a plantation owned by a Scot called Paul Cameron. Few slave houses have survived the passage of the years, as they were built cheaply and quickly, but these are large and well constructed, built by the enslaved people themselves. They have stone foundations, and each has a large fireplace and chimney made with bricks moulded from clay dug from the nearby creek. And there are marks in the bricks, small hand and footprints. Child's prints. It was the children's job to make the bricks. These prints tell the visual story of the people who sat around that fireplace at night, voices barely heard above a whisper by the rest of the world.

•◆•

In the biggest and finest house on the old plantation in North Carolina lived three bears. Brer Bear, Mama Bear, and Baby Bear, and these bears were so plump. They had trained all the animals in the forest to bring them food, seeds and nuts and berries, and they ate everything, until they were so plump they couldn't move, so they spent all day and all night in their great big bed, and still they grumbled.

One morning, there was a-knocking on the door.

'Who's that disturbin' my sleep so late at night?' said Brer Bear.

'It's Sister Skunk. I hear you bears are a mite squashed in, and I'm a mighty fine housekeeper, and I reckon I could make this little old house the pleasantest and most sweet-smelling house in the whole of North Carolina.'

'We ain't got no room for a housekeeper. Go 'way, we don't want none o' your sort round here,' shouted Brer Bear.

But Mama Bear elbowed Brer Bear and said she could do with a housekeeper to help with the chores.

So Brer Bear opened the door and Sister Skunk walked in, took a look around, sniffed the air, and said she could make this the pleasantest house in North Carolina, and she let rip with one of her very special smells. Well, Brer Bear and Mama Bear and Baby Bear took one whiff of Sister Skunk's stink, and they rolled out of bed and ran out the door faster than old Brer Rabbit.

Sister Skunk moved in. She lit the fire and filled the room with flowers, and she made that house the pleasantest and most sweet-smelling house in the whole of North Carolina, without those smelly old bears. And she felt free for the first time in her life.

And those old bears? Well, I hear they're still runnin' from the stink that Sister Skunk kicked up!

And they gonna be runnin' till the smell goes away.

•◆•

The story of the Stagville plantation is well documented. There are papers and letters in the North Carolina State Archives and in the Southern Historical Collection at the university in Chapel Hill, written by the Cameron and Bennehan families who ran the plantation. Paul Cameron was a state senator who became the wealthiest man in North Carolina. The history of the 900 enslaved people remains in the footprints in the walls, and in the force of the spoken word, the oral stories, 'Nommo'.

In the 1770s, before the abolitionist cause took root, William Williams Pantycelyn translated the life stories of a number of slaves into Welsh. The first anti-slavery publication written in Welsh was by Morgan John Rhys, who emigrated to Savannah, Georgia, in 1794, helped establish the Welsh settlement of Cambria in Pennsylvania, opened an African–American church, printed pamphlets exposing Jamaican plantation owners, published the first account written personally by an enslaved man, David George, and campaigned on behalf of native people. Samuel Roberts, Montgomeryshire writer, poet, pacifist, and reformer, emigrated to Tennessee, wrote the story of Yamba the Slave Girl, and was condemned during the Civil War when he accused the North of fighting for reasons other than the abolition of slavery.

Iolo Morganwg, self-styled 'rattleskull genius', bard of liberty, father of the Gorsedd, poet, radical, stonemason, flautist, and collector of folk tales, railed passionately against slavery. Iolo enjoyed sugar in his tea, but he placed a sign in the window of his free-trade shop in Cowbridge saying he did not sell sugar from the West Indies for fear it was produced by slave labour. Instead, he only sold sugar produced by free men. One sign read, 'East India Sweets, uncontaminated with human gore'. Iolo refused to trade with his three brothers, who owned plantations and slaves in Jamaica. He displayed a copy of Tom Paine's banned book, *Rights of Man*, in his shop window. When two government officials bought it and attempted to arrest Iolo for selling subversive literature, they discovered it was a copy of the Bible, for where better to find the rights of man?

Iolo wrote many animal fables, 'crittur tales', to explain his beliefs.

• ◆ •

A frisky wild horse lived in the woods of Glyndaronwy, black as the night he was, with a shaggy matted mane and no shoes to his feet. He lived as free as the birds, grazed where he wished, rolled in the dust of the forest floor, and leapt into the air just because he could. One morning he galloped to the border of Dolgynon, and there he saw an old piebald carthorse, grazing on dew-covered grass, drinking freshwater from a silver stream and fenced-in safely in a clover meadow.

Wild Horse stared. He thought how foolish he had been all his life to live in the scary wild forest and eat nothing but sour grass and drink from muddy puddles, when he could live in a flower-filled meadow, drink silver water from a spring and smell fragrant clover. So he decided to leave behind the wild horses of the woods and live with this cultured horse of the fields.

Wild Horse took a running jump, leapt over the fence and landed in the meadow. Old Carthorse looked at him, shook his plaited mane and asked him, whatever was he thinking? Wild Horse told him he had decided to live a life of comfort and splendour in a flower-strewn meadow with servants to wait on his every whinney. The wise old carthorse snorted, and told him it was far better to be free in the forest than be imprisoned in a meadow, unable to escape the shackles of his own life.

But Wild Horse did not listen, and soon the owner of the meadow found him, chased him with bear-dogs and bloodhounds, threw nets over him, bridled him and pack-saddled him, taught him to pull carts, and whipped him if he disobeyed.

For the rest of his life, Wild Horse hauled timber to make fences, cut from trees felled in the woods where he had once roamed free.

• ◆ •

Among the 'critturs' were a flock of black sheep. Cadwaladr Owen, a Quaker from Bala, bought and sold slaves in Philadelphia in the early 1800s. The James, Jones, and Harry families of the Welsh Tract in South Carolina brought slaves from Delaware. Three Welsh indentured slaves were advertised as having run away from Robert Williams, a planter from near Charles Town. One of them, Jenkins James, spoke 'very much Welshy'. In 1744, Williams also offered a reward for another runaway he called Thomas Edwards.

Richard Pennant, First Baron Penrhyn and MP for Liverpool, was fiercely anti-abolitionist and an outspoken champion of slavery, who believed banning the traffic of Africans would be economic disaster for the country. He also ordered his managers to ensure that his slaves were encouraged to raise children, as he reasoned it was cheaper to 'breed his own' than buy new ones. He even paid midwives bonuses for delivering live babies. Penrhyn Castle has stood for 200 years as a monument to the forced transportation and enslavement of African people.

Then there was the curious story of the son of William Wells, a rich Cardiff merchant who emigrated to St Kitts, where he ran several plantations and fathered children with six enslaved women.

In September 1779, a slave named Juggy gave birth to a boy she named Nathaniel. William Wells granted her freedom and she changed her name to Joardine Wells. Nathaniel, however, was raised in slavery until he was 9, when he was freed and sent to Cardiff and London to be educated. On his father's death in 1794, Nathaniel inherited the family plantations and used the wealth to buy Piercefield House in Chepstow, where he created a giant's cave, a grotto, a lover's leap, and a druid's temple, all in keeping with the late Georgian desire for the sublime and picturesque. He married twice, firstly to Harriet Este, the daughter of King George's former chaplain, and on her death, to Esther Owen, and in all fathered twenty-two children. He hunted with the Chepstow hounds, became a Justice of the Peace, the first black High Sheriff of Monmouthshire, and the second black man to be an officer in the Yeomanry. In 1822, as Lieutenant Wells, he was ordered to

break the picket lines of striking miners and iron workers, and was relieved of his commission shortly afterwards.

In all this time, Nathaniel never returned to St Kitts and took little interest in the abolitionist cause. He left managers to run his plantations, although he intervened to order the release of his mother's family. In the 1820s, he ignored a critical report that condemned his estate managers for exceeding the maximum thirty-nine lashes allowed as punishment to enslaved people. When slavery was abolished in 1833, he insisted on compensation for his loss. Four years later he was paid a mighty sum of money by the government.

When Nathaniel Wells died in Park Street, Bath on 13 May 1852 at the age of 72, Piercefield House was left to fall into ruin, and his land eventually became Chepstow Racecourse. His memory leaves the smell of a tale told by the supporters of slavery to give credence to the idea that everyone would be a slave owner if only they had the money and power.

However, the weavers of Carmarthenshire didn't necessarily agree:

•◆•

At Nant yr Hebog, the old farmer had died and left the business to her son and his partner. However, they couldn't find the old woman's savings, so had no money to keep the farm running. One night the son had come home after drowning his sorrows in the pub, when he saw someone standing on top of the muck heap, a huge pile of manure and dung that was fermenting like a fine wine in the farmyard. The figure looked exactly like his dead mother, with a beaver hat tied to her head with a red and yellow-spotted scarf. He rubbed his eyes and looked again, and she was still there. He called her name, she turned and vanished. He ran inside to tell his partner that his mother was standing on top of the muck heap. She rolled her eyes, smelled his breath, and told him to keep off the cheap beer.

Next night he came home from the pub and there was his mother again, on top of the muck heap, kneeling down as if she were planting something. He hurried inside to fetch his partner, and this time they both saw the old woman before she vanished. They climbed up the muck heap, and there on the very top was a little ring of hen's feathers. They stared at each other. This was a sign that there was something under the heap, and they knew it was sensible to listen to the birds. They started digging with their bare hands, deep down into the muck, till they were smeared from head to foot, and what do you think they found? Yes, gold. The old woman's savings.

So they opened a woollen mill at Drefach Felindre and employed all the weavers for miles around to make cloth, which they sold to America. Welsh Plains, they called it, otherwise known as Negro Cloth, which was made into simple clothes by the enslaved peoples. They took the rest of the money to the bank, and the smell when they walked through the doors was pungent. The tellers stuck dolly-pegs on their noses, and stuffed the money into the vaults and closed the door as quickly as they could.

And the money slowly passed from hand to hand and bank to bank, and it spread around the country and then the world, and that's why every international financial transaction to this very day still carries the smell of the old Carmarthenshire muck heap.

In Search of
Fanny the Barmaid

(Being a journey across the visible walls and invisible boundaries of Wales and America in the year 2016, adapted from its first publication by the author in Planet *the Welsh Internationalist, No. 225.)*

When the Provincetown Playhouse opened in bohemian Greenwich Village in November 1916, the first two plays performed were *King Arthur's Socks*, by Floyd Dell, and Eugene O'Neill's *Bound East for Cardiff*, which told of a British Tramp Steamer, *Glencairn*, caught in fog halfway between New York and Wales. One of the crew, Yank, lay broken in his bunk after a fall, desperate to reach Cardiff before he passed over to the otherworld.

• ◆ •

YANK: You know Fanny the barmaid at the Red Stork in Cardiff?
DRISCOLL: Sure, and who doesn't?
YANK: She's been good to me. She tried to lend me half a crown
when I was broke there last trip. Buy her the biggest box of candy
yuh c'n find in Cardiff. (breaking down – in a choking voice).

•◆•

Almost 100 years later, in the spring of 2016, I was sat by the
banks of Llyn Eiddwen on Mynydd Bach, thinking about the story
of the red-haired lady who lives in the lake with her herd of milk-
white cattle who can be seen at dusk grazing on meadowsweet at
the water's edge, the boundary of their world. I heard footsteps
squelching through the mossy ground behind me, and a lady with
bottle-red hair, wearing a multi-coloured hooped jumper, black
leggings and wellies, sat down next to me, pulled out a tin, offered
me a fairy cake, and said, 'What you doin', love?'

So I told my red-haired companion about the red-haired lady
who lives beneath the water. She wiped the crumbs from her
mouth with her sleeve, bellowed with laughter, shook her bottle-
red head, and said no lady could ever live in Llyn Eiddwen. 'It's full
of leeches. She'd be eaten alive.'

She said, 'Go on, tells us a proper story'. So I told her a tale from
Ifan Griffiths, folk poet and agricultural worker from Llangristiolus
on Ynys Môn.

•◆•

Ifan lived with his mother in a cottage in Llangristiolus, and she
told him he was never to cross the boundary, and that boundary
was the church wall. On the other side was a flower meadow, and a
deep dark wood, and a cave where the fairies lived. Ifan knew that
the fairies stole little children and kept them for a year and a day,
and sometimes never returned them at all. He loved to hear stories
about the fairies, but he never wanted to meet them.

It was Christmas Day on Ynys Môn, and Ifan's mother gave him a penny pistol, one that fired caps and made a bang. That morning he shot the congregation on their way to morning service; he shot the vicar, several dogs and the church cat. He found himself on the other side of the boundary wall. He walked across the hoar-frosted meadow, through the deep dark wood where black branches tugged at his hair, and there in the mouth of the cave were the fairies. Four of them, two large and two small, sat around a great trestle table, their hunting dogs with red tongues lolling from their mouths, ears pricked as if waiting for an order. The smell of roast potatoes, pheasant, chicken, and turkey filled the air. Ifan dropped his pistol, for what was the use of a gun in the face of the fairies?

A girl and boy, the same size as Ifan, ran up to him and round him in circles. The boy stopped and pointed to a button on Ifan's shirt, and when Ifan looked down, the boy chucked him under the chin. The girl drew her hand across his cheek. She had crow-black hair, deep eyes, and dark skin. He was very young, but he fell head over heels in love with her. She told him her name was Juliana, and all that morning they played, then he joined them for Christmas dinner.

Juliana's mother explained in Welsh that her husband was from a faraway land called Scotland, and she was from another dream-world called the Mediterranean. They were itinerant agricultural workers, there to mend fences and repair stone walls. In the spring they would move on. Ifan remembered his mother was expecting him for Christmas dinner, but before he left, Juliana asked him to return to play with them. She kissed him on the cheek, and he didn't wash for a month.

He returned every day to play, and soon he had given over the idea that they were fairies. When spring came, they left, and Ifan longed for Juliana, for at least a month, until she slipped from his mind completely.

Years passed, and at the end of the Great War, Ifan was working in a canteen in an army camp in Dunkirk, making meals for soldiers bound for the front, and those returning, shell-shocked and

broken. He bought meat and vegetables from the local farmers, a job that suited him perfectly, for he was born with a story on his lips, and he could talk with them in their own language.

One winter's day, an old woman and her daughter walked into the camp carrying a basket of trinkets, and asked whether they could sell their necklaces, earrings and brooches to the soldiers as keepsakes. Ifan said he could do better than that. He placed a trestle table at the entrance to the camp, and each day he brought them mugs of tea, and enjoyed their company. The old woman told him stories, although the girl was always quiet.

On Christmas Day, Ifan brought them a roast dinner, and the old lady told him she spoke every language in Europe, and not just Spanish and French, but Catalan, Occitan, Cornish, Galician, Frisian, Scots and Irish Gaelic. He bet her he spoke one language she couldn't speak, and she replied, 'Rwy'n siarad Cymraeg' and she showed him a postcard of a sign on a railway platform: 'Llanfairpwllgwyngyllgogerychwyrndrobwllllantysiliogogogoch.'

Well, Ifan's mouth opened, his hand shook, and he spilled his tea. This was where he lived. Then the daughter spoke. 'You lived with your mother in the cottage beyond the boundary. I used to watch you from behind the church wall. You came to play. Oh, I loved you.' Ifan's jaw dropped to the ground. Crow-black hair, deep eyes, dark skin, it was Juliana. They had wandered round Europe, from one country to another, always moved on, marginalised and dispossessed. They lost their menfolk and found themselves at an army camp in Dunkirk at Christmas, as it was when Ifan and Juliana first met.

When the war ended, Juliana pleaded with Ifan to come with them. He didn't know what to do. His mother was waiting for him. He couldn't disobey orders. After he was shipped home, he had no address to write to, so he never knew what happened to Juliana. This wasn't a movie. Or a fairy tale. It was Ifan's encounter with the fairies.

• ◆ •

In 1776, on his way to Pwllheli, the antiquarian and traveller
Thomas Pennant also encountered the 'fairies'. Their names were
Mary Bach and her brother Dic, dwarfs who were housekeepers
to a local gentleman in Penmorfa. Some 240 years later, I was following Mr Pennant's footsteps around Pen Llŷn, where the gaps in
the stone walls are patched with rusting wrought-iron bedsteads,
signposts mysteriously turn in the night to confuse visitors, and
Cowbois Rhos Botwnnog sing sweet country and west-Walian
to the birds. It was Referendum Day 2016, and the people were
about to vote on whether to leave the European Union. It felt as if
I was about to meet the fairies, too.

A handwritten sign in the cobbler's shop in Pwllheli stated,
'It's about Islamisation safeguard your children your spouse your
culture your life vote leave.' The shop was closed, there was no
punctuation, or any Muslim hordes marching down Gaol Street
to steal children and keep them for a year and a day. I caught the
bus to Bryncroes and spent the afternoon drawing the farmhouse
near Sarn Meyllteyrn where Moses Griffiths, illustrator of Thomas
Pennant's travel books, spent his childhood. I called at a polling
station and listened to a young schoolteacher who knew his friends
in the farming community were about to vote to leave Europe as
a protest against too much paperwork, regardless of their reliance
on EU agricultural subsidies. I followed the advice in the cobbler's
window, and left. For America.

On 25 September, I found myself standing on the stage of the
Provincetown Playhouse in Greenwich Village where, 100 years
before, Yank had lain on his bunk in the Glancairn, crossing
the foggy boundary to visit Fanny the Cardiff barmaid. Eugene
O'Neill had stood on this stage when he acted as one of the crew
members in his own play in 1916. Edward Albee and Sam Shepard
had written for the Playhouse, and Marlon Brando had trodden
these boards as a fledgling actor. These were names from a very
different Mabinogi to mine.

The Greenwich Village storyteller Regina Ress had invited me to the Provincetown Playhouse to join her to tell stories about the visible walls and invisible boundaries that were occupying the minds of politicians in advance of the impending American election. Regina took me to Reggio's cafe, one of the last of the old beatnik haunts, where Bob Dylan and Joan Baez hung out. There is a painting on the wall by a pupil of Caravaggio, hanging next to the world's oldest surviving cappuccino machine. I sat at the same table as Carey Mulligan when she lays into Oscar Isaac for getting her pregnant in the Coen Brothers film *Inside Llewyn Davis*.

Reggio's was a quiet refuge from the hysteria that was sweeping the country. New Yorkers were wide-eyed in disbelief at the thought of 'that man' becoming president. I walked to Fifth Avenue to see Trump Tower for myself. The wall was emblazoned with a giant fried egg, a banana telephone, and a huge skull. It felt as if walls were tumbling down.

Back at the Provincetown, Regina entranced the audience with migratory tales from her travels to Mexico and South America. I told the story of the red-haired lady of Llyn Eiddwen, and explained how so many Welsh fairy tales are about meeting those from the other side of the boundary, and whether to offer a hand of friendship or keep them out. An elderly pink-haired Brooklyn lady growled, 'We don't have any lake ladies here. Y'know why? The alligators ate 'em all.'

YANK: This sailor life ain't much to cry about leavin' – just one ship after another, hard work, small pay, and bum grub; and when we git into port, just a drunk endin' up in a fight, and all your money gone, and then ship away again. Never meetin' no nice people; never gittin' outa sailor town, hardly, in any port; travelin' all over the world and never seein' none of it; without no one to care whether you're alive or dead. (with a bitter smile).

•◆•

I left Liberal America and followed the trail of hope towards Appalachia, but rather than walk across the Allegheny Mountains with my belongings tied to a pack mule, I booked a dollar ticket on the Westbound Megabus to Pittsburgh. The driver pulled in for a rest break at a Mexican diner in Pennsylvania. At the entrance was a pile of bricks, with a handwritten sign, 'Trump needs to finish this wall, Hillary needs a-rrest'.

Appalachia is a land of few farms, dense forest, derelict mine workings, and mountaintop removal, where people express themselves through folk arts, quilt making, and traditional pottery. There are few fairy tales here, except in the liars' competitions.

Houses aren't separated by fences. It's not considered polite. I asked my West Virginia cousin, how do the neighbours know where the boundaries are? 'Oh, they know. Step over one. You'll find out.' The American Invisible Fence Company has designed a wall of unseen lasers to keep dogs within their gardens, without having to insult the neighbours by erecting a wall. There is an invisible fence between Appalachia and New York, as tall as the tales, constructed of wealth disparity and misunderstanding.

Before the enclosures in Wales, the sheep knew exactly where the boundaries were on the mountains, and had no need of walls or fences or silly old sheepdogs.

•◆•

A young couple lived in a ramshackle lime-washed cottage at the foot of a mountain, with their baby boy who had never spoken a word. One day, they sat him by the front door. He stared at the mountain, picked up a stone, turned it over in his chubby hands, polished it with spittle, and placed it on top of another stone. Day after day, he piled stone upon stone. It was no surprise to anyone that he grew into a strong and silent young man who earned his living as a stonewaller.

People remarked how straight his walls were. Then one day, they heard shouting, followed by a crash. They clambered up the mountain to find part of his wall had collapsed on top of him. He had argued with the stones over where the boundary should be. They dug him out and carried him home, and although his body was broken, his parents cared for him, and he slowly mended. They sat him by the front door to feel the sun on his face. He stared at the mountain, raised his arm, and despite the pain, picked up a stone, smelled it, stroked it in his palm, polished it with spittle, and placed it upon another.

Soon he was stonewalling once more, and as he grew older his walls became less straight. They were full of bends where the stones refused to do what he wished, wobbles when he dreamed of the barmaid in Y Tafarn Vic, and gaps where the tylwyth teg refused him access through their unseen land.

• ◆ •

I finished my travels in Pennsylvania, in a small town not far from the gentrified old steel and coal city of Pittsburgh, where Andy Warhol was born. There is a huge multi-storey gallery of his work, where the staff are easily mistaken for exhibits. Outside, there are statues of the Pittsburgh Pirates baseball team. The Welsh came here in droves. One was a dyn hybys, a cunning man, John D. 'Bonesetter' Rees, who manipulated the torn and strained muscles of the miners and steelworkers, for if they were off work injured, they didn't get paid. Rees's reputation led him to become the first chiropractor to the Pittsburgh Pirates. There is a statue to him in Youngstown, Ohio, and his nickname was adopted by the most famous of bonesetters, Dr Leonard 'Bones' McCoy of the Starship Enterprise.

I was here to tell Welsh fairy tales in the Central Presbyterian Church in Tarentum on the Allegheny River. Here was the familiar story of the closure of the steelworks, unemployment, homelessness, alcohol and drug abuse. Minister Bob Dayton has

opened up the doors of the church to anyone in need, and has an imaginative way to attract and entertain his congregation. He presents puppet shows based on Welsh folk tales and mythology, with Rhiannon, Branwen, Bendigeidfran, and even Dylan Thomas, complete with a cigarette dangling from this lips and a half-empty bottle in his hand.

When I got home in January 2017, I told these stories in Y Drwm in the National Library of Wales. It was a perfect way to end the project, but it soon became apparent that I'd hardly begun. We live in a world where walls fall down, boundaries move, and conflicts are endless. I was staring into a bottomless hole.

•◆•

The Griffiths boys, Dai and Twm, had heard all the stories of beautiful women who lived in the lakes of Wales. They knew about Llyn y Fan Fach, Llyn Barfog, Llyn y Forwyn, Llyn Fanod, the old millpond at Felin Wern, and Llyn Eiddwen, and that these ladies rose out of the water and married young farmers, without any of that birds and bees nonsense. All you needed to do was wait until one of these girls appeared covered in pondweed, and there we are.

Their father told the teenage brothers that a red-haired girl lived in their old farm pond, and he advised them to be careful, because she might be American. Well, this only encouraged them. They liked country and western music. Twm could play the harmonica, and Dai was a dab hand at the comb and paper. Every evening they kept watch by the pond for Dolly Parton to appear, although it occurred to them that she might smell given that the pond was stagnant and covered in duckweed, having never been cleaned in years. But they knew America was at the bottom of the old farm pond, and they were partial to a bit of Johnny Cash.

Well, they waited, and time passed and Dai and Twm Griffiths never married, and the joke was that they were still waiting for their American lady of the lake. Truth was they were so busy running the farm, they never had time for dating. And Father

hadn't taught them how to talk to a lady, which Mother said was just as well, 'cos he was rubbish at it.

Don't get me wrong, they did have girlfriends when they were younger, but it was always the girls who made the first move. Dai was engaged once, because Annie Davies told him so. They went on a pre-wedding honeymoon to Barmouth, and when she suggested they should go on a second one he said no, so she asked him why and he said he hadn't thought much of the first one.

Twm was saving up to get married, although he didn't know who to ask, until Sian Post agreed to accompany him to Butlins in Pwllheli. They stayed in their room for a week, and when she asked him what he was thinking about, he told her he was working out how to fill in the form for the EU milk subsidy. She giggled, tickled him, and hit him with a pillow, until she realised he was deadly serious.

Hopeless. The pair of them. Slow, not at all impulsive, and always ready with a joke to avoid commitment. Their lives were all cows and sheep, fencing and roofing, shearing and tractors, the annual Young Farmer's pantomime, and sniffing their socks as they dried by the hearth. There was no time for anyone else.

And suddenly it was all too late. Their teeth and hair were falling out. All they had to amuse themselves was flirting with young Ceri on the checkout at Morrisons, who always called them her lovely boys. She told them her boyfriend had given her a bucket, and they asked if it was metal and she said no it was red plastic, so Dai offered her one made of aluminium. She thanked him, called him her lovely boy, and he told her she would never be alone with a proper bucket.

So, there they were, two old red-cheeked men, dewdrops on the ends of their noses, standing by the pungent old farm pond, on the boundary of their world, wondering if their father's story was true, and whether America was at the bottom of their pond, and that one day they might marry Dolly. Though they were practical boys – they would be satisfied with someone who looked like her.

The pond was coloured with diesel rainbows. A collection of beer bottles had accumulated around the edge as memories of too many lonely nights. Beneath the surface were great diving beetle larvae that had eaten all the tadpoles and sticklebacks, and picked the bones clean of a few lambs and chickens who had fallen in. Dai was convinced no lady could live in there. Twm wasn't so gloomy. Maybe it was cleaner at the bottom?

They looked at each other, open-eyed. The bottom? They realised they didn't know how deep the pond was. The Loch Ness Monster, or Teggy, or Ginny Greenteeth could be down there. Dai dropped a stone, and watched it sink, and they listened. Nothing. They tried a bottle filled with sand. Same. Perhaps this was a bottomless pond. The gateway to Nashville.

So they took a brick, tied a long rope around it, and lowered it slowly into the water. It disappeared below the duckweed – down it went, with cries of 'Careful now', and 'don't drop it on her head'.

Dreams of their sweet Tennessee lake lady flooded their minds. They would share her, like they always shared a beer. They would take her to the cattle sale with one of them on each of her arms, then escort her to the Llew Du for a cwrw where they would buy her pork scratchings. She could sit between them on their old roofless Massey Ferguson, and they would sleep three-in-a-bed, though they would have to oil the squeaky springs.

They reached the end of the rope, yet it was still tight in their hands. The brick hadn't touched the bottom. That rope was 50ft, maybe 100? The pond must be bottomless. So they hauled up the brick, hand over brown-blotched hand, and when they lifted it out of the water, they couldn't believe their eyes. It was bone dry.

They scratched their heads, and then the extraordinary truth dawned. The brick must have travelled all the way to Arizona, where it had dried out in the hot desert sun.

So off they went to Morrisons to tell young Ceri that they were leaving for America, where they were going to marry someone who looked not unlike Dolly Parton, and Twm was going to play

harmonica with Johnny Cash, and all they needed was diving gear and a pre-packed lunch.

Ceri sold them a couple of cheddar and mango chutney sandwiches, blew them a kiss, and told them she would see her lovely boys tomorrow.

YANK: S'long, Drisc!' (He stares straight in front of him with eyes starting from their sockets.) 'Who's that?
DRISCOLL: Who? What?
YANK: (faintly) A pretty lady dressed in black. (His face twitches and his body writhes in a final spasm, then straightens out rigidly.)

• ◆ •

Yank never made it to see his Fanny. He crossed the boundary to the otherworld. Which was a shame. He might have become a farmer, filled the gaps in the stone walls with rusty wrought-iron bedsteads, built a bottomless pond, and played banjo with Cowbois Rhos Botwnnog.

As my cousin in West Virginia said, fussing her old dog, 'We are all mutts.'

13

The Devil and the Mothman

I n 1924 the Great Western Railway published a small book of Welsh and Cornish folk tales, *Legend Land*, with illustrations by the Czech artist Willy Pogany. Londoners could pick up a copy at Paddington and catch the train to the wild west of Britain, visit the Lady of Llyn y Fan Fach, meet the old woman who crossed the Devil's Bridge, and join the orgy with the Queen of the Fairies at Pennard Castle. In 2017 Visit Wales unknowingly revived the idea with Flwyddyn Chwedlau, Year of Legends, which included Cerys Matthews opening an exhibition that featured Margaret Jones's exquisite paintings from Y Mabinogi at the National Library, installing a 25ft-tall puppet of Bendegeidfran in a nearby art centre alongside work by David Hockney and Bedwyr Williams, and recreating the drowning of the submerged land of Cantre'r Gwaelod on a catwalk on the seafront in Aberystwyth, complete with the walking zombie dead and a fireworks display.

•◆•

Back in the late 1700s, folk tales were attracting tourists to
Ceredigion. The land around Pontarfynach, the Monk's Bridge,
was a wild place of sheep farms, spoil heaps, and mine buildings,
where people clung to the hillsides by their fingernails. Land
was being enclosed, men were press-ganged into the war with
Napoleon, and bellies ached with hunger. Into this impoverished
world came Thomas Johnes, aesthete, moral philosopher, MP for
Cardigan, and author of *A Cardiganshire Landlord's Advice to his
Tenants*. He inherited the nearby Hafod estate, built a romantic
home in this cold Ceredigion valley, and planted 3 million trees,
larch and pine on the uplands, oak and beech below. Every tree
and stream was designed to be more sublime than nature herself,
with waterfalls blasted through rock with dynamite, and grottos
and caves designed by architects and draughtsmen. The *White
Book of Rhydderch* (*Y Mabinogi*), had been written down by monks
at nearby Ystrad Fflur almost 500 years before. Turner came to
paint. Coleridge passed through without stopping. An unnatural
wilderness grew from a natural wilderness.

Megan Llandunach was standing on top of the gorge above
Pontarfynach, gazing at the waterfalls of Hafod far below, clutch-
ing a piece of string attached to a shabby mongrel, and weeping
into the wind, when she became aware of a man behind her. She
turned and there stood a monk, dressed in grey robes with a hood
pulled over his face so his eyes shone from the shadows. She looked
down at his feet. They were cloven.

He spoke, 'Why do you cry so, my dear?'

She dried her tears and wiped her nose, 'Because my wayward
cow has wandered to the other side of the gorge, and I am too
weak and feeble to climb down to fetch her.'

The Devil, for it was he, offered to build her a bridge, providing
she gave him the soul of the first living creature that crossed over.
She wiped a dewdrop from her nose, while the Devil dreamed of
beef for dinner. He gathered stones from all parts of Wales and
Ireland, and soon a fine bridge spanned the gorge. He proudly

showed it to Megan, expecting praise. Instead, she whistled her cow to stay, pulled a stale loaf from her pocket, threw it across the bridge, and her shabby mongrel followed it eagerly to the other side. The Devil threw his head back, exposed his white skull and deep eye sockets, and let out a howl that made the river freeze over. Then he shuffled off, with the soul of a shabby mongrel on a piece of string trailing behind him.

In the late 1700s the name of the village was changed from the Monk's Bridge to the more exciting Devil's Bridge, to attract visitors to the newly built Hafod hotel. And it worked. Tourists came to stay and were fleeced by the housekeeper, who overcharged them for wandering around the ruins of Thomas Johnes's Hafod Mansion after it burned down in the early 1800s. The construction of the Vale of Rheidol narrow gauge railway in the early 1900s enticed more people, and now the story is told on an interpretation board outside the railway station, so that visitors can read it for themselves before calling at the chocolate shop, so removing the necessity to employ a storyteller.

• ◆ •

At Point Pleasant, West Virginia, where a great silver bridge spanned the wide Ohio River, a Mothman was sighted in November 1966. Those who saw him (or her – I doubt anyone really knew) described it as being 7ft tall with a barrel chest and a piercing shriek, 10ft-high bat-wings and huge, red, glowing eyes. Mothman was seen twenty-six times over the following year, in all by over 100 people. As sightings increased, so did reports of other strange phenomena. Telephones stopped working, police dispatch radios scrambled, televisions went crackly, cars lost power, and there were numerous reports of UFOs. Some thought that Mothman was a mutant, spawned from the local chemical and weapons dumps. Some said it was an owl or a sandhill crane, while those with long memories knew it was 'the Curse of Chief Cornstalk'.

In 1774, three years after the battle of Point Pleasant, the Shawnee were being forced off their land. Hokolesqua (Cornstalk) went to Fort Randolph to negotiate peace. He sought to maintain his tribe's neutrality, yet he was arrested and kept in a locked room. On 10 November, after an American militiaman from the fort was killed nearby, angry soldiers burst into Hokolesqua's room and shot him dead, along with his son Elinipsico, and two other Shawnee men.

As he lay dying, eight bullets in his body, Hokolesqua said he had saved his people from harm, had been the border man's friend, had only gone to war to protect his lands, had refused to join with the red coats, and for his loyalty he and his son had been murdered. He called on the Great Spirit to curse the hopes of the people, that they be paralysed by the stain of his blood.

Since then there have been mine disasters, tornadoes, train crashes, aircraft have fallen from the sky, and on 15 December 1967, a year after Mothman's first appearance, the Silver Bridge that connected Point Pleasant to Kanauga on the Ohio side of the river collapsed during the afternoon rush hour, killing forty-six people. Some claimed the catastrophe was triggered by a sonic boom from Mothman's wings, others believed that Mothman had been sent to warn the people of Point Pleasant to avoid the bridge. Whatever the truth, Mothman was never seen again.

But it didn't disappear from memory. In 1975, New York writer John Keel, one of the paranormal investigators drawn to Point Pleasant, published *The Mothman Prophecies*, which became a feature film starring Richard Gere and Laura Linney. On the day the film opened, West Virginia's secretary of state announced that Point Pleasant's old KFC would be converted into a Mothman visitor centre. The first Mothman festival was held, the local park was renamed Mothman park, and a 12ft-tall stainless steel sculpture of the folk hero was unveiled. Its red eyes were meant to light up at night, but sponsorship funding ran out, although it is convenient for taking selfies.

In 2005 the Mothman Museum opened across the street from the statue, where you can buy Mothmanabilia, T-shirts, books, DVDs, plush dolls, comic books, hats, licence plates, and bags of Mothman droppings, which are meant to be eaten rather than used as compost.

There is also a memorial to Hokolesqua. A large stone obelisk stands by the river in Point Pleasant Battlefield State Park, containing his surviving remains, three teeth and a few fragments of bone, sealed in the centre of the obelisk, perhaps to ensure that his curse is safely locked away.

• ◆ •

In the early 1200s, Llywelyn the Great and his wife Joan, daughter of King John, were living at Aber in Gwynedd with their baby boy. Llywelyn kept a pack of hunting dogs and he loved one of them as much as his own child. Gelert was gentle as a lamb, whiter than a swan, stronger than a lion, faster than a tiger, and was always at the head of the pack when the horn sounded. No wolf had escaped Gelert's jaws for six years.

Llywelyn and Joan had tucked the child safely in his wooden cradle by the hearth in their hunting lodge, then set off on a hunt. They killed three wolves, and blew their horns to call the dogs to return, but Gelert did not appear. Llywelyn feared his favourite hound had been slain.

They returned to the hunting lodge to find Gelert lying by the overturned cradle, blood dripping from his chops and caked to his fur. Thinking Gelert had slaughtered and eaten his child, Llywelyn ran his sword through the dog's heart. He went to the cradle and saw, lying dead on the flagstones, the body of a huge wolf. He lifted up the cradle and there was his son, safe and sound. The gruesome truth dawned. Gelert had knocked over the cradle to hide the baby, and fought off the wolf. Llywelyn stroked the dying hound, while Gelert licked his hand. He buried the dog near the river, placed a slate slab over the grave, and the village became known as Beddgelert, Gelert's Grave.

This story was thought to have been brought to Beddgelert from South Wales in the late 1700s by David Prichard, landlord of the Goat Hotel, to encourage tourists to visit the village and part with their money. By 1800, the story of the Faithful Hound had gone viral, popularised by the poem, 'The Grave of the Greyhound', written by William Spenser during his stay at the Goat that same year. And the phrase 'As Sorry as the Man who Killed his Greyhound' was used to describe anyone who made assumptions before thinking. And for 200 years people have flocked to the little village in Snowdonia to visit Gelert's grave.

My dad told me the dog wasn't buried there at all, that it had all been a scam by Landlord Prichard to encourage visitors to book a room at the hotel for the night, and persuade them to part with their money in exchange for pints of 'Faithful Gelert Ale' and tea towels with picturesque engravings of the town. In other words, the story had been invented to bring economic growth by fleecing the tourists. This appealed to my dad's sense of humour.

However, there is another version of the story that was known long before Landlord Prichard and the Welsh tourist authorities realised the faithful hound had potential as a money earner. The 'Fabula de Beth Kilhart' was written around 1592, and tells of how Llywelyn and Johanna Notha brought a dog from England that 'excelled the Swan, or the snow in whiteness, the lamb in gentleness, the tiger in swiftness, and the Lion in strength of jaw and courage, whose name was Kill-hart'. They chased a hart (a stag) across Gwynedd, and in the resulting fight the hart and dog killed each other. The dog was buried at 'Bethkilhart'. This story was said to have been taken from an early thirteenth-century manuscript, raising the intriguing thought that Llywelyn may have told this story about himself.

•◆•

On 12 September 1952, a group of boys were playing football in Flatwoods, Braxton County, West Virginia, deep in Appalachia, when a long tubular light passed across the sky and fell to earth beyond the hillside above the May family residence. Kathleen May and two of her boys and their dog went to investigate.

They made their way through woods that were so familiar to them, approached the top of the hill where the fireball had landed, and saw two powerful beams of light pierce the darkness. There was a sickening metallic odour in the air that made everyone feel nauseous. They shone a flashlight and saw a large machine-like creature, bigger than a man, with two bright flashing eyes.

The monster metal man had a red face and bright green clothing, which hung in folds below the waist. Its head was shaped like the ace of spades and it had two long arms with three long fingers. It looked like an alien, or a secret government weapon, or a flying saucer from a 1950s B movie, and there was a foul stench in the air. There was no time to think. Mrs May and the boys ran for their lives through the woods, presuming the monster was right behind them.

The dog approached the creature, tilted its head to one side, whimpered, barked, cowered, curled its lip, then ran home, where it threw up on the porch. In the morning, all that was left was a lingering odour, two large skid marks, and some trampled grass.

The newspapers published eyewitness accounts, drawings of the monster, and interviews with the survivors. And then they reported that the poor dog had died. There was an outpouring of grief, and more newspapers were sold.

However, the monster had not chased the children. It was nothing like the drawings in the press, and the poor dog was very much alive, if a little nauseated. All the boys saw was a light, a crash, and a metal thing; they smelled a smell, they were frightened, and they ran. Some said it was an owl, but the story had taken on a life of its own, and Flatwoods had its own Frankenstein's monster.

It emerged later that a New York couple were driving through Flatwoods on the evening after the monster was seen, when they smelled something pungent. They stopped the car and opened

the bonnet, and then started screaming. Behind them was the monster, all green with red flashing eyes and as big as a house, so they jumped back in the car and crouched on the floor in terror as the creature rattled the windscreen. The following day they found three lines of burn marks on the paintwork and windows.

The Flatwoods Monster never appeared again after that. Except in drawings, postcards, action figures, flashlights, books, comics, T-shirts, mugs, tea towels, and home-made life-size figurines. It celebrated its fiftieth anniversary with a community festival; there is a Monster Museum in the visitor centre, and a sign proclaims, 'Welcome to Flatwoods, Home of the Green Monster'. A forty-five-minute documentary made by local film-maker Seth Breedlove attracted over 200 people to the community cinema in nearby Sutton when it received its world premiere in the spring of 2018. The cinema had never sold out before, so they hurriedly arranged another screening for those who were left outside in the street with nothing else to do on a Saturday night in small-town West Virginia.

The Flatwoods Monster is helping revitalise the local economy, and the county has taken it to heart, although the guys in the visitor centre were more interested in telling the story of the Braxton Goat. No supernatural aliens or conspiracy theories here, just a farmer's billy goat that likes to sit on a rock above the road and watch the motorists drive by on their way to who-knows-where. A few days before this, a farmer near Arthurdale gave me a lift, and on the back seat of his pick-up was a small white goat. I asked where he was taking the goat, and he said, 'Nowhere, she just likes going for a ride in the afternoon.'

But my road trip with the Arthurdale Goat is a whole other story.

• ◆ •

The tales of the Flatwoods dog and Gelert's dog, the Devil's Bridge and the Mothman's Bridge, have taken on lives of their own – not only because they are rattling good yarns, but because they earn a few bucks for the neighbours.

I want to believe. And that ain't ... oh, you know.

14

Owl-Women
and Eagle-Men

Back in the old Welsh Dreamtime, the birds decided to elect a king. They called a parliament, and they came from north and south, big birds and little birds, and they agreed their king would be the bird who could fly the highest. They knew Eagle would win, for he could soar high over the mountains of Eryri. Eagle flew higher than any other bird till he could fly no higher, when a little wren who had been hiding amongst his feathers jumped from his back, flew just that little bit higher, sang as loudly as she could, and landed back on Eagle.

Wren had become king, and the birds were furious. How could they have elected such a cheeky little loudmouth as their king? They decided to drown her in their own tears. They took it in turns to weep into a pan until it was full, but clumsy old Owl knocked it over and spilt the tears, so they chased her away, and cursed her to fly by night to escape their anger.

Wren was smart, and she understood she would not be a popular monarch, so she abdicated in favour of Eagle, happy that a little bird with a loud voice could be heard above all the presidential twittering.

•◆•

Among the Eastern Cherokee, Golden Eagle was the most beloved bird. She was War Eagle, and she had the prettiest feathers of all the birds, so pretty that her tail was worth as much as a horse. No one dared hurt Eagle, or she haunted their dreams – except for one man, the Eagle-hunter. He was allowed to hunt her for her feathers, but only in the winter after the crops had been gathered and the snakes had gone to sleep. Then, Eagle-hunter went into the mountains alone, left a deer tied to a post, and waited for Eagle. He fired an arrow, took her feathers, and went to the village to receive his blood money, when there would be an eagle dance.

One summer, a hunter in the mountains had hung a deer on a drying pole. In the night, he heard the sound of the wind, the flapping of wings, and he saw Eagle eating his deer. So he shot Eagle and took the deer back to the village to eat. When the elders heard what he had done, they knew there would be trouble, so they collected the feathers and that evening held an eagle dance. At midnight a strange warrior entered, dressed in eagle feathers, and she told stories about her adventures. Then she whooped, 'Hi!' and one of the eagle dancers dropped down dead. Seven times she told stories and whooped, until all the dancers were dead. She told them she was taking revenge for her eagle sister's death, but everyone knew this was Eagle herself.

• ◆ •

In Wales, King Eagle grew old and wise, but his wisdom had turned him into a gloomy old soul. So, he decided to cheer himself up by marrying Owl, but he only wanted to marry her if she was as ancient as himself. But how would he know? It would be rude to ask her age, and she might peck him with her sharp beak. So he decided to ask his ancient friends for advice.

Eagle flew to see the Stag of Rhedynfre in Gwent. He asked Stag if he knew how old Owl was.

Stag said, 'See this withered old stump of an oak tree? An oak is 300 years growing, 300 years in its prime, 300 years decaying, and

300 years rotting into earth. When I was a fawn, this tree was an acorn, and Owl was a wrinkled old bird. But if you don't believe me, there is one much older than I. Ask the Salmon of Llyn Llaw.'

Eagle went to see Salmon and asked if she knew how old Owl was.

Salmon said, 'See the number of scales and spots on my back, add those to the spots on my belly, multiply them by the number of grains of spawn in my body, that's how old I am, yet when I was a fry, Owl was a wrinkled old bird. But if you don't believe me, there is one much older than I. Ask Ousel of Cilgwri.'

Eagle found Ousel sitting on a pebble, and asked how old Owl was.

Ousel said, 'See this little pebble? It was once so huge that 300 of the strongest oxen could not pull it. I have cleaned my beak upon it once every night before going to sleep. I have no idea how old I am, but I have only ever known Owl as a wrinkled old bird. But if you don't believe me, there is one much older and wiser than I. Go to the bedevilled bog of Borth, and ask old Toad. He gibbers incomprehensibly and is as wrinkled as a walnut, but he is older and wiser than the very earth itself. If he does not know the age of Owl, no one does.'

Eagle flew to Cors Fochno, and found Toad sitting in the middle of the swamp, breathing and blinking. He told Toad that he was marrying Owl, but only if she was unimaginably ancient. So how old was Owl?

Toad blinked and breathed, and said, 'I only eat dust. And I never eat half enough dust to fill my belly. See those hills? I have eaten all the dust in the valleys of Wales, though I have only eaten one grain a day, for fear I eat all the earth before my death. That would not be sensible or sustainable, now would it? You see, I am as old as the rocks, yet when I was little more than a tadpole, Owl was already a wrinkled old harridan, forever shrieking, 'ty-hwt-ty-hwt', all through the long winter nights, frightening the children, boring the ancestors, disturbing my sleep. Marry her, and take her away with you. Dimwit. Dimwit. Dimwit.'

So Eagle married Owl, and all the animals in Wales came to the wedding, all except for Toad. Maybe he forgot, or he fell asleep, or

maybe you should ask him? He's still there, in the middle of the quivering bog of Borth, the wisest creature in Wales, smarter even than the bards. But if you try to walk out across the peat, you'll be sucked down into the deep dark depths long before you reach him.

Listen, he's still there. Talking to us. 'Dimwit. Dimwit. Dimwits.'

• ◆ •

Owls are perceived as portents of death, hated by all birds, punished by being banished to the night. They are otherworldly, archives of wisdom, with morals unlike ours. They screech and hoot, speak a different language, like migrants from a strange land.

A Cherokee widow advised her young daughter only to marry a man who was a good hunter. So when a hunter came to call, she followed her mother's advice and married him. On the next day he went out fishing and came home late at night with only three small fish, saying he would have better luck tomorrow. But the following night he came home with two worthless sand lizards, and on the third night all he had were some scraps cut from a dead deer. She told her mother her husband was a poor hunter, and her mother told her to follow him and see what he got up to. So next day, she tracked him through the woods to the river and watched him turn into Uguku, Hooting Owl. He flew over the water, scooped up some sand, and pulled out a crawfish. She ran home and waited for him with her arms folded. He showed her the crawfish and she asked why he had caught no fish. He said Owl had frightened them away. She said, 'I think you are Owl,' and she chased him out of the house, and he pined away till there was no flesh left on his body apart from his head.

This story was recorded in the late 1890s by the journalist and ethnologist James Mooney, who was living amongst the Eastern Cherokee in North Carolina. Mooney was collecting folk tales, creation myths, and cultural beliefs for the Smithsonian in Washington DC, which published his epic, *Myths of the Cherokee* in 1902. He acknowledged that three-quarters of his information

came from one man, A'yûn'inï (Swimmer), a doctor and herbalist who spoke and wrote only Tsalagi, and kept notebooks containing the traditions and tales of his people. Mooney called A'yûn'inï, 'a genuine aboriginal antiquarian and patriot, proud of his people and their ancient system.'

•➖•

In the epic fourth branch of the Mabinogi, the conjurer Gwydion had stolen his sister Arianrhod's son and was raising him alone, perhaps because he was the father. Arianrhod refused to name the boy, so Gwydion tricked her into calling him Lleu Llaw Gyffes, but she cursed Lleu never to be able to marry or love a woman of flesh and blood. So Gwydion took the flowers of oak, meadow-sweet, and gorse, and conjured up a woman made of flowers to offer to Lleu. He named her Blodeuwedd, and although she was no object (she had feelings and emotions of her own) you cannot give a flower a conscience. She had an affair with Gronw Pebr, and the lovers hatched an elaborate plot to kill Lleu. Gronw pierced Lleu with a spear and he transformed into an eagle. Gwydion found his eagle-son and nursed him back to health. Lleu took a spear and hurled it at Gronw, who protected himself with a slab of slate held in front of his chest, but it pierced the slate and his heart. Gwydion punished Blodeuwedd by turning her into an owl, cursed forever to live alone in the darkness of night.

Artists and writers have found themselves mesmerised by Blodeuwedd's eyes and trapped beneath her talons. Count just a few of them: Robert Graves, Alan Garner, Margaret Jones, Alan Lee, Ceri Richards, Harri Webb, Saunders Lewis, Gwyn Jones, and any number of Victorian romantic painters, contemporary theatre groups, creative writing scholars, and performance artists. She is the star of a full-length animated film, has her own bottled beer and artisan dolls, and endless internet images portray her as a goddess, images she would surely shred in her beak if she could. There is a sense that she has been torn from her roots.

Blodeuwedd grew out of the landscape of Snowdonia. You can walk to the site of Lleu's castle at Tomen y Mur, to the lake where her handmaidens drowned at Llyn y Morwynion, and to the banks of the Cynfal where a farmer has erected a large slate slab with a hole in the middle, which is unlikely to be the one that Gronw held up to protect himself from the spear that pierced his heart. However, although the woman of flowers has firmly rooted herself in Wales, the woman as owl also occurs in Oklahoma.

• ◆ •

In 2012, the Cherokee scholar Christopher B. Teuton published a collection of folk tales from the Turtle Island Liars' Club. Teuton presents the stories in the context of conversations between four elders from the Western Cherokee in Oklahoma who tell tales to explain their place in the world. They are told over a drink on the front porch, where the personal lives of the tellers and their friends mingle with the fictional characters and their narratives. Words change with each telling, so even their own creation myths develop over time. History transforms to tell the stories of tomorrow.

There was debate over whether the tales should be told outside the culture or written down at all, and quite understandably so, given the way native cultures have been appropriated throughout history. However, the Oconaluftee Cherokee in North Carolina take their bear dance around folk festivals, and storyteller Lloyd Arneach tells tales sensitively to those outside his culture. In Wales, performance storyteller Michael Harvey has found a way to present the story of Blodeuwedd to theatre audiences, while keeping rooted in the Snowdonia landscape.

So, this story of Owl-woman was told by Hastings Shade, fisher-man, smith, tradition bearer, deputy chief of the Cherokee Nation, and member of the Turtle Island Liars' Club, who has been celebrated since his passing in 2010 with an annual informal festival that bears his name.

• ◆ •

Cherokees are afraid of owls. They bring bad luck, maybe death. But you have to remember an owl is only a bird.

Anawegi helped her mother and brothers and sisters look after their log house and care for her father who was ill. When he fell sick, he taught her how to hunt, for she was the oldest and cleverest. She noticed that whenever her father fell into a fever, owls gathered around the house. Her mother told her they were aniskili, the ones who could turn themselves into other things, who fed off the weak and sick.

One evening Anawegi made her father some soup, and as she was about to feed him, an owl flew into the room and circled the bed. As she chased the owl out of the window, she noticed it had two strange stripes on its head. When she ran back to her father, he had passed to the otherworld. They buried him four days later, near the house, as was the custom.

Time passed and times were hard, and Anawegi hunted, using all the skills her father had taught her, and his spirit lived on in his daughter. But there were few rabbits to hunt, so she went further into the wood, and her mother told her not to stay out after dark or Owl would get her. And Owl watched her, in the form of a bird.

And Owl said to Possum, 'I like this girl. She is strong and clever. I will have this girl.' For Owl was once human, but he had hurt himself.

One morning a young man walked into the yard, holding a rabbit. 'This was all I could get, but I will bring more tomorrow.'

They invited him to eat, but the sun was rising and he said no. She noticed he had a cloth tied around his head.

Next morning he returned with more rabbits. And so this went on. And Anawegi said to her mother, 'He is a fine hunter.'

And her mother said, 'He hunts by night, no one hunts by night.'

And Anawegi said, 'No, he must hunt by day, then sleep at night, and visit in the morning.'

Her mother nodded, knowingly.

And Anawegi said, 'I like this man. He is clever and strong. I will have this man.'

Next morning, he brought a deer, and the family feasted, and he asked for Anawegi's hand. For a marriage amongst the Cherokee in those days, the man had to offer venison, and the girl accepted with a gift of ears of corn. That night he came for Anawegi, and she placed the corn in his palm, and removed the cloth he wore around his head. And there were the two strange stripes she saw on the owl the night her father died, and she knew he had killed her father. She rushed forward to attack him, but one of his arrows was pointing out of his quiver, and it pierced her belly. As she fell back, he told her he had not killed her father, he was merely a messenger sent to escort him safely to the otherworld. His arrows had been given to him by a medicine man, who said he must be careful never to draw blood from them. One day he cut himself and was turned into an owl. And now Anawegi would become an owl, too, like Blodeuwedd before her.

They married, but neither changed into human form again. They became the Moon-Eyed People. And that is why at night you will hear two owls, ker-wick, ker-whoo. Don't be afraid, they are only messengers. For we must listen to birdsong, just like our elders once did, and be wise in whom we elect to be our kings.

15

Hoodoo and Healers

I t was Grandmother Spider who brought light to the Cherokee Nation. Before then, everything was dark. Sun lived on the other side of the world and never showed herself to the people, who lived like moon-eyed moles in the dark.

The animals decided someone must go and talk to Sun, and persuade her to shine her light on the people. Buzzard flew towards her but burned her feathers. Possum tried climbing up the trees but singed her tail. Coyote leapt into the clouds but set fire to her fur. Then Grandmother Spider spoke up, and said she knew how to capture the sunlight.

She travelled to the east and placed a clay bowl in the centre of her web, and then squinted her eyes till she lined up the bowl with Sun. When Sun fell into the clay bowl, she took hold of it and traced her way back home to the west, following the lines of her web, taking the light with her. Sun carried on around Grandmother Spider's web on to the east and back to the west. Every day she did this, and so the sunlight came to be shared all around the world.

Grandmother Spider was the first woman to use her powers to help the people. She was the first of the Grannies. They call us Granny Women in Appalachia, Gwiddanes in Wales, Atsasgili in Cherokee. But we are not of the hubble-bubble kind. No cauldrons or pointy hats. You wouldn't spot us in a crowd. No one

knows our real names, only the words they call us by. Wolf, owl, cat, bear, toad, dog, snake, fox, crow, raven, coyote. We came from the east with Sun and travelled to the west along Granny Spider's web. We carry the blood of old worlders, settlers, and natives in our veins. We are from Cymru and Keetoowah.

We are sisters. There are three of us.

In Appalachia, I am Annie. A Granny. A black cat. A Southern lady, a country belle who never said, 'Thank you, kind sir.' I am no delicate flower in a lace bonnet. I'm tough as old leather boots, held together by the blood in my veins. I'm in my first flowering. Fresh faced and freckled, hair as black as a raven, although one day I will be as wrinkled as a mouldy grey peach. I can divine for water, read tea leaves from a porcelain cup, vanish warts and heal wounds, I can do hoodoo, and I'm a God-fearing girl. When I want to be.

In Cherokee, I am Ana. Anawegi. An owl. Coyote. Raven. Spider. I fly by night. I am daughter of the weed mother, I know how to boil up my sisters, how to make tinctures and potions. But don't be fooled by my dark plaits and red lips, I am a war-woman as much as peacemaker. Men need me to be their conscience. I can stand up to the medicine men. I can make babies, and hold them to my breast while I throw a spear at a jackrabbit. I am feathers and teeth and bones.

In Cymru, my name is Anna. A hare. Crow. Toad. Another dark girl. I leave poisoned apples for unsuspecting children, I make love potions and mischief, I can stop horses with a whisper, prevent butter from churning, tell the future with little more than a pin and a yarn of wool. I run rings around the dyn hysbys, the cunning man. When I grow wrinkles, I'll wear a tall hat and sit outside a mud-walled cottage and charge tourists a penny for my photograph. I can make a doll, and pierce it through the heart with a pin.

•◆•

Anna lived with her mother Liza in a ramshackle hut with a cor-
rugated iron roof on the beach near Llanfairfechan, between the
high-tide mark and the cliff face. There were no boundaries in
their world, so they paid rent to no man. The sea came into their
home whenever it wished, so they climbed the ladder to the crog
loft and slept with the chickens till it left.

They kept themselves alive by begging for bread, milking wild
goats, and borrowing a turnip or a cabbage from a farmer's field.
Liza wasn't Anna's blood mother. She opened her door one morning
and there was a baby in a basket on the doorstep. She thought it
had been left by the travellers, and was wondering whether to give
her to a family, when she saw a sparkle in the baby's eyes. So she
raised the child as her own daughter. As Anna grew, she learned
to love the kindness of her foster mother. Old Liza had looked
after her own mother all her life, and although many saw her as a
fearsome old hag with a sharp tongue, to Anna she was her crow
mother. Her blood mother.

They knew all the witch women. There was Dolly Llewellyn,
the queen of the Pembrokeshire witches, who once cursed a couple
who refused to offer her a lift in their pony and trap, and as she
watched them trundle down the road, the wheels mysteriously
fell off. Beti Grwca from Ceinewydd was famed for making love
potions, and once gave them to two babies who were doomed to
fall in love when they grew, whether they wanted to or not. Beti'r
Bont turned a servant at Dolfawr into a hare and chased him as a
greyhound, then transformed him into a horse and rode him all
night long. The old hag of the Black Mountain chased little girls
while croaking as a black crow, while the old hag of Cors Fochno
breathed on children till they shook with fever. Poor Hannah from
Llandudno was just different, so they burned her alive in a cave on
the Great Orme. Betty Foggy once stopped a ship being launched
in Pembroke Dock. Mari Berllan Pitter from Pennant could stop
horses with a whisper, made a waterwheel turn backwards, and
could curse anyone except Lluestr the local poet. Creaky Wheel
of Llanbadarn Fawr stole potatoes in the middle of the night and

if anyone complained, she threatened to break their heads with a sickle while her daughter put the evil eye on them.

One day, Liza visited Carreg Fawr and asked the farmer for a little food in exchange for some lucky white pebbles she had collected from the stream. Seemed reasonable enough, but the miserable man set one of his hunting dogs on her. Anna screamed, Liza jammed her foot between the dog's bared teeth, wrapped her shawl around her daughter's shoulders, and kicked the dog off. She ran for their lives, with the dog gnawing at her ankles. When she reached home, Liza held Anna and stroked her black hair and told her it would be alright. She made a comforting bowl of soup with a couple of potatoes she had borrowed from the farmer's vegetable patch, and sang lullabies till Anna closed her green eyes and drifted into dreams.

That night, Liza found herself in a dark place. She scooped up some clay from the stagnant pool and mixed it with a little moss from the graveyard. By the light of a rush candle, she moulded it into the shape of the farmer, clothed it in bloodied fox fur, and stuck two ivy berries on its face for eyes. With moonlight pouring through the window, she heated the figure on a griddle over the fire, muttered a spell, mixed in a little blood from the dog bites on her leg, took her hatpin, and pierced the doll through the heart. At Carreg Fawr, the farmer stopped stroking his dog, wiped his forehead, scratched his chest, and carried on hunting. For Liza meant no harm to any living soul, and the spell was toothless without intent.

She had learned how to make a doll from old Elen Dahl, one of the Llanddona tribe over the straits on Ynys Môn. Elen had been washed up on the beach with the rest of her people in a boat with no oars. They were cast afloat to die in the storms as punishment for something, probably for being women. The locals tried to push them back out to sea, yet still there was no riddance of them. They built homes on the edge of the village, always on the edge. Old Elen was tough as boot nails, small with red hair, and one of her sisters, Siani Bwt, had two thumbs on her left

hand. She rented a room in Caernarfon once a week, where she told fortunes, with old clothes draped over a string to keep her consultations private from the waiting crowds. That's where she taught Liza how to make a poppet.

Elen explained that poppets only worked if you intended hurting someone. She had stuck pins into many a poor soul. All her sisters could do this, but it once backfired on Big Bela, who had cursed a man called Goronwy Tudor who had a birthmark above his breast that he believed protected him. Nonetheless, his dairy became afflicted, the milk dried up, the cows gave blood, and he saw a hare suckling at their udders. Goronwy knew this hare was Bela, so he shot it with a silver coin and it ran screaming. He followed a trail of blood over the green hill to a cottage, where he found Bela with a wound in her leg. She threw a curse at him:

'Crwydro y byddo am oesodd lawer,
Ac yn mhob cam, camfa,
Yn mhob camfa, codwm,
Yn mhob codwm, tori asgwrm
Nid yr asggwrm mwyaf na'r lleiaf,
Ond asgwrn chwil corn ei wddw bob tro.'

So Goronwy collected some witch's butter from decayed trees, moulded it into a likeness of Bela, and stuck it with pins. Every pin caused her to scream with pain and blood to flow, until she released Goronwy from the curse, and he gave her the poppet to destroy.

Well, time passed and Anna's blood started to flow, and she let her hair out of plaits. That autumn, Liza passed over to the other-world, and Anna was left an orphan girl again. Neighbours were kind: they brought her bread and milk and gave her paid work, sewing and darning, but at night she was alone with her thoughts. With each passing evening, the thoughts darkened, till they were black as peat. Anna remembered how cruelly the farmer at Carreg Fawr had treated her mother.

By the light of the rush candle, she took Liza's clay doll, added scrapings from the body of a burned rat, feet and limbs of a toad, white quartz from the cliff for bones, weeds for sinews, mountain

herbs mixed with saltwater worms, pine gum, the heart of a black cockerel, clay from the river bed, water collected from a waterfall by moonlight, and ivy berries for eyes. She breathed on it, passed it through the night air, heated it in the fire, doused it in the stream, pierced it with the hatpin, muttered a curse, smiled, and threw it into the fire. At Carreg Fawr, that mean farmer choked, clutched his chest, dropped his lantern, and set fire to the hay in his barn. Next morning the neighbours found only a smouldering blackened skeleton.

No one suspected Dark Anna. Why would they? She lived her life as a beggar girl, unseen and unloved, never betraying her emotions to anyone. She carved pegs from elder wood, carried them round in a wicker basket, and sold them for a penny. In six months the elder softened and the pegs broke, so she visited again and stared into her customers' eyes until they bought more. She wrapped some of the pegs in scraps of cloth torn from her mother's old frocks, cut a notch at the top which she filled with fox fur for hair, drew eyes and a mouth with her fingernail dipped in blood, and sold them as peg-dolls. Children loved them and screamed till their parents bought them. It was never wise to refuse to pay her or send her away without food, for she knew how to whittle a likeness.

There we are. That's Dark Anna from Llanfairfechan.

• ◆ •

In Appalachia, she calls herself Annie, but it's not her real name, it's after her Grandma Lacy Ann. They lived at Booger Hole on Big Otter Creek in Clay County, in a ramshackle old schoolhouse made of logs, with quilts hung over the windows to keep the wind and mosquitoes out of their hair. They grew corn and tobacco, kept a few chickens and an old piebald mare called Fannie, and Granny clenched a clay pipe between her teeth as she sang hymns to a pump organ she kept on the porch. Annie had a baby sister, and her own baby was waiting to be born. Soon the Boggs family

would have another mouth to feed, and she would be lain in the cradle by the fire and wrapped in a piece of quilt. There are notches carved in the end of the cradle, a reminder of each of the poor childer who died there.

Granny was small and wrinkled round the mouth and wore a scarf to hide the scars on her neck. She had the power to take sicknesses away, warts or pimples, cows not giving milk; she cured them all, children or animals, just by touching them. She brewed potions out of ginseng that could make someone fall in love with you, and another that stopped your bones aching. And she swore by sodey. If Annie had a poorly belly, Granny mixed sodey in a glass of water, she rubbed it into cut knees and poured it into all her cooking: sodey in beans, sodey in biscuits, sodey in groundhog, sodey in chicken. And she had another potion that she painted onto her warts, and then she cut them out with a needle. Oh, Annie screamed like a stuck pig.

One day a man called Andrew Sampson came calling and asked if he could borrow Granny's old horse, Fannie, to help with the ploughing. Now, Granny felt she had to be polite to a neighbour, but she didn't like 'Hooch' Sampson. She called him the Boogieman. When he brought Fannie back, she was worn out and covered in burrs, so Granny told Boogieman she'd hex him till his eyes watered. Next morning he woke up covered in burrs, swearing he'd been turned into a horse and ridden all over Pilot Knob by Granny.

Booger Hole was a lawless place, shootings were common, and the law was a joke. One of the respectable folks, Old Man Cottrell, said that Granny was a witch, 'cos she rode him all night long, and left him shivering and sweating. He called her Mother Boggs. Truth was, Granny took no nonsense from these men who were always fighting. She wouldn't hold her tongue, so she made enemies. And there was another reason. Annie was seeing one of Cottrell's boys, and he didn't want a witch-girl for his daughter.

There were lots of Grannies in West Virginia. Old Ma Heaton from Flemington went to church only once, on the day it burned

to the ground. Mrs Williams of Hoodsville, Monongalia, gave her next-door neighbour's husband the belly ache till he near burst. Mandy Main hexed Jim Bradford till he died and she was able to buy his land. Sarah Thorne of Bunner Flats turned into a wild beast and tore folks limb from limb. Martha Pringle was a racoon-witch, at least till she got shot by a silver bullet. One old Granny hexed another by bending a darning needle in half till the old lady bent double in pain. Zubinka Lovic lived an hour from Austria and cured all ills just by the laying on of her big hairy hands. Old Lady Harris counteracted curses on milk, and spat tobacco through a hole in the floor, though she often missed, so there was a pile of dried rotten smelly tobacco that she never cleaned up. She kept a dead cow hung up by the hooves, and when it had well and truly rotted she beat it with a stick until the jelly entrails slithered to the ground, then she fried it up and ate it, and swore it cured all ills and kept her healthy.

One morning, a man called Henry Hargis was found riddled full of bullets, and they said he'd been killed for his money, 'cos he kept his dollars hidden under the floorboards, in the pig sty, and up the chimney, for he didn't trust banks. Well, Granny thought she knew the name of the man who had done it.

So she cast a spell on the man's horse. It had always been tame, but now he couldn't catch it. He begged Grandma to take off the spell and she agreed, providing he told her where Henry Hargis was buried. He glared at her and said he'd string her up by the neck, and she said he'd be forever cursed. So he took her to Henry's grave and she lifted the charm.

Not long after, the womenfolk were all gathered in a room, stitching and quilting and drinking liquor. Granny got into an argument with her neighbour, Rosa Lyons, over who killed Henry Hargis. She lit her clay pipe and told Rosa that she knew who had done it, and before her tobacco was smoked, she could show her where Henry was buried. Annie was there with her newborn baby and she tried to hush Granny, but it was too late: nothing was going to stop her shooting off her mouth.

That night, Annie was asleep in bed when she heard a gunshot and the sound of two people running away. She came downstairs and found her poor Granny sitting in her rocking chair by the fire, with her arms hanging down and blood dripping onto the dusty wooden boards. Old Man Cottrell and one of his boys were arrested and charged with murder, but he was acquitted 'cos they had no evidence, and they thought Granny had witched him. And anyway, it wasn't him who shot Granny.

Annie knew who'd done it. And why. Granny knew too much, you see. She had crossed some powerful men in the town. Men with connections to the chemical works in Charleston who had made a lot of money on the backs of the poor folk who had to breathe in all that sulphur.

A few years after Old Man Cottrell had been acquitted of Granny's murder, Rosa Lyons and her brother Fred Moore were arrested on suspicion of killing both Granny and Henry Hargis. Seems they suspected Old Mother Boggs knew too much, and that's why they shot her.

Thing is, Rosa didn't shoot Granny either, although Fred was involved. Annie knew who had done it, everyone did, but if you spoke up in Booger Hole you'd be shot, too. And Annie couldn't say anything, for she had her little baby at her breast, and she didn't want him left with no momma.

A few years later, Hooch Sampson and his son Howard were arrested for burning to death a man called Preston Tanner. Rosa and Fred's brother James were arrested, too. While they were awaiting trial, a poster went up around town:

> We the citizens of Clay county seeing that we cannot get justice by law, have organized the Clay county mob. We have pledged our lives to drive these people from our county or kill them. If we cannot catch and hang you, we shall sneak upon you and kill you as you killed Henry Hargis, Lacy Ana Boggs, the old peddler and Preston Tanner. If before you leave there is any stealing, killing or burning, we will get bloodhounds and detectives and

run you to the ends of the earth. Bill Sampson, Kooch Sampson, Fred Moore, and Aaron Runyon are hereby notified to leave the state in ten days. Rose Lyons, Bill Moore and Elizabeth Sampson are notified to leave in thirty days.

A few days later, several buildings were blown apart with dynamite, and the Sampsons were run out of town, all thanks to the Clay County Mob.

Now folks come to Annie for help, 'cos they know she has all Granny's medicine and potions and all her charms and cures. If they ask her to release them from curses, she says, 'sure', and she draws a heart on the ground, or on tree bark, or on a piece of 'tater sacking, then she takes all the pins and needles from her darning tin, and she pierces that heart till it bleeds. Never fails. Granny learned the trick from an old lady called Agnes Dolan, and taught it to Annie, and she'll pass it on to her baby girl.

That's her, Annie Boggs from Big Otter Creek.

•◆•

Then there's Ana, half-owl, half-blood Cherokee, and she's just moved to Asheville, North Carolina, where she's studying art at the college. You can call her Little Blue Fox. She has a Cherokee name, too, but she won't tell it you. That's between her and her people. Ana lived with her Granny Lucy till she was 18, and she learned lots of stuff about plants and potions and the natural world, and it was Lucy who told her all about her Granny Gore.

Nancie Gore was a full-blood Cherokee who married a settler by name of Tipton Gore. She walked from her homeland in Tennessee with Tipton and his two children, a family called Philibert, and two enslaved people, and they settled in a quiet neighbourhood called Owens Bend in the Ozark Mountains, so peaceful you won't find it on the map. Tipton scouted for the Confederates during the Civil War, while his eldest boy James fought for the Union.

When he died, Nancie Gore only had time to wrap him in a quilt and bury him in a cardboard box near their house.

Now, there are two things you need to know about Granny Gore. She loved horses, and she hated doctors. She had her own methods and remedies, passed down from the old medicine men she knew. People came from all over North Carolina and Tennessee to visit her. Some of her healing methods are so simple, you wonder why doctors don't use them. She grew all kinds of herbs and yarbs, and had all sorts of cures and charms, but no curses, mind. Granny didn't do cursing.

If you got the chills, she gave you Wahoo Tea. A bad cough was cured with wild cherry bark, or skunk oil, mixed with mutton tallow, goose grease and turpentine, applied to rags and laid on the chest.

Stomach ache was sorted with a syrup made from a tablespoon of sulphur, five tablespoons of sorghum, and a pint of peach brandy. If that didn't work, she tried goldenseal and the linings of chicken gizzards. Ginseng tea was for stomach cramps, button snake root tea for colic, and if you needed your bowels clearing, sienna leaves and catnip worked a treat as a laxative, while horehound killed worms in the gut.

Then there was catnip tea for sore neck. Skillet bark tea kept your heart beating. Oat tea stopped you scratching measles spots. Flax seed poultice for boils. Yellow root for canker sores. Elderberry tinctures helped you live longer. Sassafras tea thinned the blood, while bloodroot stopped bleeding at childbirth, and black pepper or cobwebs helped a scab form over a cut.

Raw Irish mashed potatoes, placed on the skin, drew out splinters of wood or glass. Pith from goose quills for kidney troubles. Pyorrhea of the gums was eased by burning a red corn cob to cinders, then cooling it and rubbing it on the sores.

Granny once prescribed skillet bark tea to a blue baby who couldn't breathe. Dr Lloyd, a man with a medical licence, had given up saving the baby, but after Granny gave it a few drops of skillet bark tea, the next morning, the baby had its colour back

and was breathing. Dr Lloyd took some of the concoction back to his lab for tests and found it was pure cortisone.

Granny lived a healthy life; she always helped the sick and the poor. She was 96 when she died a peaceful death in 1917, and she's buried in a pine coffin in the new Philibert Cemetery.

And now old Granny's twice great-granddaughter, Little Blue Fox, is taking up her tradition of using yarbs to heal folks. Lots of folk are following these ideas here in Asheville. Lots of women, anyways. They're marrying the old herbal concoctions and folk beliefs with natural remedies and healthy eating. Ana can cure the common cough with an elderberry potion mixed with root beer or liquor. And she gets to sing on the streets with Abby the spoon lady – she is just the best. It's all good here, though there may be a few too many hippies and craft beards, but see through the sparkle and glitter, and there's memories of the old Granny ways.

Granny Lucy told Ana another story, and Ana tells it in her way, not how it was told to her, for that's the way things are done round here.

Nûñ'yunu'wï, Stoneskin, was a great big cannibal monster with flesh of solid stone. He carried a cane made of bright, shining rock, which he pointed in the air, smelled the end, and pointed it in another direction, until he finally smelled human flesh. Then he moved slowly, very slowly, with the help of his cane, until he came to a village, where he gobbled everyone up.

Once, he reached a river and pointed his cane and smelled the end, and he knew there was a camp on the other bank with lots of juicy humans to gobble up. He threw the cane into the air and it formed a bridge of bright shining rock over the river. He crossed slowly over the bridge and when he reached the other side, it became a cane again. As he walked slowly towards the camp, you could hear the tip-tap-tap of his cane.

A hunter was watching, and he came running into the camp and told the medicine man he had seen Stoneskin coming, and they would all be gobbled up. There was panic, and the medicine man knew there was no way to kill the monster with

the skin of stone. Then young Medicine-girl spoke up and said she knew how to be rid of Stoneskin. All she needed were seven woman who were bleeding, because Nûñ'yunu'wï, strong man that he was, could not look upon a menstrual woman.

So seven women came forward and Medicine-girl told them to stand in a line and take off their clothes. They stood there, all shapes and sizes, all bleeding, some heavily, one young girl just beginning. Medicine-girl placed her at the back of the line, hidden from view. Soon they heard the tip-tap-tapping of Nûñ'yunu'wï's cane, coming through the woods. He came up to the first woman and he dribbled and licked his stone lips, then he smelled the blood and he retched and told her she was unclean. He came to the next woman and this time he gagged. He reached the third woman and now he was vomiting. He staggered past the fourth, fifth, and sixth women, and he was throwing up blood, and his steps grew weaker until he came to the last girl, who was menstrual for the first time. He opened his mouth and she saw his sharp teeth, but she stood her ground, brave girl that she was, and the blood poured from Stoneskin's mouth and he dropped down at her feet.

Medicine-girl pinned Stoneskin to the ground with seven sourwood stakes through his body, and when night came she piled great logs over him and set fire to them. And as Nûñ'yunu'wï burned, his mouth opened and all the secrets of the herbs came pouring out, and he sang the hunting songs for calling up the bear and the deer and all the animals of the woods and mountains. And then he burned to ashes and there was little left other than white bones and black blood.

Medicine-girl, she smeared Nûñ'yunu'wï's blood on the seven brave girls and from that day the 'unclean' women knew the secrets of the herbs and the songs of hunting, and the women ruled the Cherokee.

And that's Ana, Little Blue Fox, Tsalagi.

•◆•

We are three sisters. Ana, Annie, and Anna, from Keetoowah, Appalachia, and Cymru. We all live beneath the same moon, we tell the same stories, and we bleed the same colour blood.

And that ain't no lie.

Bibliography

Introduction

Quotes

Benjamin Williams, reprinted in: Jones, Eirian, ed; *Mynydd Bach ei Hanes/Its History* (Blaenpennal: Cwmdeithas Hanes, 2013) pp. 56–57.

References

Conley, Robert J., *Cherokee Medicine Man, The Life and Work of a Modern-Day Healer* (Norman: Oklahoma, 2005).

Davies, Sioned, trans., *The Mabinogion* (Oxford: University Press, 2007).

Emerson, P.H., 'Origin of the Welsh', in *Welsh Fairy-Tales and Other Stories* (London: D. Nutt, 1894).

Ford, Lyn, *Affrilachian Tales* (Chicago: Parkhurst Brothers, 2012).

Medlicott, Mary, *Shemi's Tall Tales* (Llandysul: Pont Books, 2008).

Musick, Ruth Ann, *Green Hills of Magic, West Virginia Folktales from Europe* (Lexington: University of Kentucky, 1970).

Pontshan, Eirwyn, *Hyfryd Iawn* (Talybont: Ceredigion, 1967).

Salsi, Lynn, *The Life and Times of Ray Hicks, Keeper of the Jack Tales* (Knoxville: University of Tennessee Press, 2008).

Sampson, John, *XXI Welsh Gypsy Folk-Tales* (Newtown: Gregynog Press, 1933).

Stevenson, Peter, *Welsh Folk Tales* (Stroud, History Press, 2017).

Teuton, Christopher B., *Cherokee Stories of the Turtle Island Liars' Club* (Chapel Hill: North Carolina Press, 2012).

Williams, Taliesin, *Iolo Manuscripts* (Llandovery: William Rees, 1848).

Wolf-Girl Visits Wales

References

Mooney, James, 'U'tlûñ'tă/Spearfinger', *Myths of the Cherokee* (Washington: US Bureau of American Ethnology, 1902).

Musick, Ruth Ann, 'Ears can give you away', *Green Hills of Magic* (The University Press of Kentucky, 2015).

Musick, Ruth Ann, 'Ivan', *Green Hills of Magic* (The University Press of Kentucky, 2015).

Musick, Ruth Ann; 'The Black Cat', *Wisdom and Witchery in West Virginia Folklore*, published in *Traditions: a Journal of West Virginia Folk Culture* (Fairmont West Virginia, 2015).

Musick, Ruth Ann, 'The Lady Was a Werewolf', *Green Hills of Magic* (The University Press of Kentucky, 2015).

Musick, Ruth Ann, 'White Wolf', *Green Hills of Magic* (The University Press of Kentucky, 2015).

Stevenson, Peter, 'Beast of Bont', *Ceredigion Folk Tales* (Stroud: The History Press, 2014).

Stevenson, Peter, 'Huw Llwyd', *Welsh Folk Tales* (Stroud: The History Press, 2017).

Teuton, Christopher B., 'The woman who turned herself into a dog', *The Turtle Island Liars' Club* (University of North Carolina Press, 2012).

Trevelyan, Marie, *Folk-lore and Folk-Stories of Wales* (London: Elliot Stock, 1909).

Trevelyan, Marie 'Wolf girl in Wales', *Folk-lore and Folk-Stories of Wales* (London: Elliot Stock, 1909).

Thanks
Helen Edwards for the inspirational conversations, for taking the time to proofread the manuscript, and for proving that folk tales really do come true.

The Moon-Eyed People

Quotes
'The History of American Women', womenhistoryblog. com/2008/11/nanyehi-nancy-ward.html

References
Cherokee Rose, Oral folk tale.

Hutcheson, Maryleigh, 'The Cherokee Woman and her Changing Role', www.austincc.edu/pgoines/maryleigh.html

Johnson, Lloyd, 'The Welsh in the Carolinas in the Eighteenth Century' (*North American Journal of Welsh Studies*, Vol. 4, no. 1 Winter 2004).

Kelly, Anne, *Calvinists Incorporated: Welsh Immigants on Ohio's Industrial Frontier* (Chicago: University of Chicago, 1997).

Mooney, James, *Myths of the Cherokee*, (USA, 1902).

'Museum of the Cherokee Indian', www.cherokeemuseum.org

'Nanyehi/Nancy Ward "The Ghi gu a"' Cherokee Heritage Documentation Center, cherokeeregistry.com/index. php?option=com_content&view=article&id=147&Ite mid=217

'Native Languages of the Americas: Tsalagi/Cherokee Legends, Myths, and Stories', www.native-languages.org/cherokee-leg-ends.htm

'Restoring Women to Cultural Memory', Suppressed Histories Archives, www.suppressedhistories.net

Thanks
Alan Hoal, storyteller from Apex, North Carolina, for first sparking my interest in the Moon-Eyed People.

Where the Welsh Came From

'These tales were collected by me whilst living in Ynys Môn during the winter 1891–2 … they were told to me and I took them down at the time. In most cases I have done but little "editing", preferring to give the stories as told.'

P.H.Emerson, *Origin of the Welsh* (London, 1894)'

References
Constantine, Mary-Ann and Leblond, Valériane, *Rhyfel y Sais Bach,* oral folk tale.
Emerson, P.H., 'Origin of the Welsh', *Welsh Fairy-Tales and Other Stories* (London: D. Nutt, 1894).
Jones, Eirian, *The War of the Little Englishman* (Talybont, Lolfa, 2007).
Jones, Eirian ed. *Mynydd Bach ei Hanes/Is History* (Blaenpennal, Cwmdeithas Hanes, 2013).
Phillips, Bethan, *The Lovers' Graves* (Gomer: Llandysul, 2007).
Rhyfel y Sais Bach (Stevenson, Peter, and Whittaker, Jacob) 2017 [film] https://swimmingcatfilms.wordpress.com/2018/03/04/rhyfel-y-sais-bach/
'The Wales Ohio Project', www.ohio.llgc.org.uk
Welsh–American Heritage Museum, Oak Hill, Ohio.
Wil Cefn Coch, oral folk tale.

Thanks
North American Festival of Wales for inviting me to tell stories in Columbus, Ohio, 2015.
And to Cousin Mark Kemp for taking me round Chillicothe and Oak Hill.

Lone Man Coyote

References

Fenn, Elizabeth A., *Encounters at the Heart of the World: A History of the Mandan People* (New York: Hill and Wang, 2014).

Jones, Emyr Wyn, 'The Welsh Indians – A Later Chapter, *National Library of Wales Journal* (Wales: 1961) Vol. 12, No. 1.

Jones, J.J., 'The legend of Madoc', *National Library of Wales Journal* (Wales: 1942) Vol. 2, Nos. 3 and 4.

'Lone Man, and the bird that turned the meat bitter', *First People, Mandan Legends*, https://www.firstpeople.us/FP-Html-Legends/Legends-MO.html#Mandan

Madog Center for Welsh Studies, www.rio.edu/madog

Pelz, Ruth, *Women of the Wild West, Biographies from Many Cultures* (Greensboro NC: Open Hand, 1975).

Rhys, Gruff, *American Interior* (London: Hamish Hamilton, 2014).

Senior, Michael, *Did Prince Madog Discover America?* (Llwyndyrys: Llygad Gwalch Cyf, 2004).

Stevenson, Peter, and Hughes, Ailsa Mair, *The Moon-eyed People and the White Ravens* (Aberystwyth Arts Centre, 2018) https://www.newwelshreview.com/article.php?id=2256

The Bohemian Consul to Cardiff

References

'"When an American is drunk he brags, and when a Welshman is drunk he sings": American identity and the celebration of Welshness in Wirt Sikes's *British Goblins* (1880)', North American Journal of Welsh Studies, Vol. 8 (2013).

Sikes, Wirt, *Rambles & Studies in Old South Wales* (London: Sampson Low, 1881).

Sikes, Wirt, 'Rowli Pugh and Cati Jones and the Ellyll', *British Goblins, The Realm of Faerie* (London: J.R. Osgood & Company, 1880).

Sikes, Wirt, 'Shui Rhys', *British Goblins, The Realm of Faerie* (London: J.R. Osgood & Company, 1880).

When Buffalo Bill Came to Aberystwyth

References

Buffalo Bill Museum, https://centerofthewest.org/explore/buffalo-bill

Carradice, Phil, 'Buffalo Bill in Wales' (BBC, 2012) www.bbc.co.uk/blogs/wales/entries/c5eb1659-9985-368b-9b86-8a35c9834aa7

Carradice, Phil, *The Wild West Show* (Llandysul: Gomer, 2013).

Thanks

Amgueddfa Ceredigion Museum

Archifdy Ceredigion Archives

Michael Freeman

This story was pieced together after hearing the inspirational Lakota storyteller Dovie Thomason.

The Cherokee Who Married a Welshman

References

McLoughlin, William G., 'The Reverend Evan Jones and the Cherokee Trail of Tears', 1838–1839 (*The Georgia Historical Quarterly* Vol. 73, No. 3, Fall 1989), pp. 559–583.

Morgan, John, *Prince of Crime* (New York: Henry Holt, 1985).

Okwedy, Phil, *Wil and the Welsh Black Cattle* (Llandysul: Gomer, 2018).

Origins: Murray the Hump (Wigley Dafydd, Gwreiddiau) BBC, 2012.

Owen, Irvin, 'Democracy and Class Struggle' democracyandclasstruggle.blogspot.com/2012/11/us-elections-in-20th-century-gangsters.html

Stevenson, Peter, *Welsh Folk Tales* (Stroud: The History Press, 2017).

John Roberts of the Frolic

References

Chase, Richard, *The Jack Tales, Folk Tales from the Southern Appalachians* (New York: Houghton Mifflin, 1943).

Heimlich, Evan, 'Gypsy Americans', https://www.everyculture.com/multi/Du-Ha/Gypsy-Americans.html

Jarman, A.O.H. and Jarman, Eldra, *The Welsh Gypsies: Children of Abram Wood* (Cardiff: University of Wales, 1991).

Jarman, Eldra and Jarman, A.O.H., *Y Sipsiwn Cymraeg* (Cardiff: University of Wales, 1979).

Pavesic, Christine, *Ray Hicks and the Jack Tales: A Study of Appalachian History, Culture, and Philosophy* (Connecticut, Universe, 2005).

Roberts, E. Ernest, *With Harp Fiddle and Folktale* (Denbigh: Gee & Son, 1981).

Sampson, John, 'Welsh Gypsy Folk-tales "The Dragon"', *Journal of the Gypsy Lore Society* (Vol. IV, No. 4, 1925).

Sobol, Joseph Daniel, *The Storyteller's Journey* (Urbana and Chicago: University of Illinois, 1999).

Welsh Romanies www.valleystream.co.uk

Thanks:

Newtown Council, for inviting me to participate in the John Roberts Project, 2017.

Harriet Earis, for collaborating on the project and playing the music of John Roberts, learned through the oral tradition.

The Legend of Prickett's Fort

References

Bray, Greg, *Prickett's Fort* (Mount Pleasant, Arcadia, 2014).

Moore, Jack B., *The Earliest Printed Version of David Morgan and the Two Indians* (West Virginia Archives and History, Vol. 23 No. 2, January 1962).

Prickett's Fort, https://www.prickettsfort.org

Sampson, John, 'Welsh Gypsy Folk-tales "Winter"', *Journal of the Gypsy Lore Society* (Vol. IV, No. 4, 1925).

'"Westmoreland" Remarkable encounter of a white man with two Indians', in a letter to a gentleman of Philadelphia Apr. 26, 1779' *United States Magazine*, (May 1779)

Ghosts of the Osage Mine

References

Arthurdale Heritage Museum.

Blizzard, William C., *When Miners March* (PM Press, Oakland CA, 2010).

Hansell, Tom, After Coal, *Stories of Survival in Appalachia and Wales*, (West Virginia University Press, 2018).

Harris, Wess, *Dead Ringers: Why Miners March* (Gay, Appalachian Community Services, 2012).

Lewis, Ronald L., *Welsh Americans: A History of Assimilation in the Coalfields* (Chapel Hill, University of North Carolina, new ed 2008).

Mellow, James R., *Walker Evans* (New York, Basic Books, 1999).

Musick, Ruth Ann, 'Big John's ghost', *The Telltale Lilac Bush and Other West Virginia Ghost Tales* (University Press of Kentucky) 1975.

Musick, Ruth Ann, 'Big Max', *The Telltale Lilac Bush and Other West Virginia Ghost Tales* (University Press of Kentucky) 1975.

Schlosser, S.E., 'Invisible Hands, A Nevada Ghost Story', americanfolklore.net/folklore/2010/07/invisible_hands.html

Stevenson, Peter, 'Coal Giant', *Welsh Folk Tales* (Stroud: The History Press, 2017).

Stoll, Steven, *Ramp Hollow: The Ordeal of Appalachia*, (New York, Hill & Wang, 2017).

'Walker Evans, 1903–1974', https://www.metmuseum.org/toah/hd/evan/hd_evan.htm

Zinn Education Project, 'Teaching People's History', https://www.zinnedproject.org

Thanks:
Scott's Run Museum and Mary Jane Coulter for organising a story session on 2 April 2018, with Lou, Mike and Willa, and to Mark Kemp for first taking me there.

Brer Bear and the Carmarthenshire Muck Heap

References
Black History Month, 'The Welsh Abolitionists', https://www.blackhistorymonth.org.uk/article/section/history-of-slavery/the_welsh_abolitionists

Bon Vivant Online, 'Innapropriate dinner conversation: the curious case of the Cherokee Freedmen' https://bonvivantonline.wordpress.com/2011/09/19/inappropriate-dinner-conversation-the-curious-case-of-the-cherokee-freedmen

Evans, Chris, *Slave Wales: The Welsh and Atlantic Slavery, 1660–1850* (Cardiff: University of Wales, 2010).

Ford, Lyn, *Beyond the Briar Patch: Affrilachian Folktales, Food and Folklore* (Chicago: Parkhurst Brothers, 2014).

Gates, Henry Louis Jr., and Tatar, Maria, *The Annotated African American Folktales* (Harvard, University Press, 2017).

Giddens, Rhiannon, www.rhiannongiddens.com

Hamlet, Janice D., 'Word! The African American Oral Tradition and its Rhetorical Impact on American Popular Culture', *Black History Bulletin*, Vol. 74, No. 1 (Winter/Spring 2011).

James, E. Wyn, 'Welsh Ballads and American Slavery' *The Welsh Journal of Religious History*, 2007.

Lewis, J.D., 'The Welsh settlements during the royal period', *(1729 to 1755)*. www.carolana.com/SC/Royal_Colony/sc_royal_colony_welsh.html

Miles, Tiya, *Ties that Bind: the Story of an Afro–Cherokee Family in Slavery and Freedom* (Berkeley: University of California, 2006).

Morganwg, Iolo, 'Wild Horse', *Ancient Fables*, pp. 585–586.

Nathans, Sydney, *A Mind to Stay, White Plantation, Black Homeland* (Cambridge: Harvard University Press, 2017).

Schlosser, S.E., *Brer Bear's House, A Georgia Folktale*, American Folklore, americanfolklore.net/folklore/2014/12/brer_bears_big_house.html

Stagville State Historic Site, www.stagville.org

Stevenson, Peter, 'The Muck Heap', *Welsh Folk Tales* (Stroud: The History Press, 2017).

Vest, Jay Hansford C., 'From Bobtail to Brer Rabbit: Native American Influences on Uncle Remus', *American Indian Quarterly*, Vol. 24, No. 1 Winter (University of Nebraska, 2000).

Thanks

Tony Hopkins, storyteller, actor, and 'Black Cherokee', who found his personal identity in New Zealand.

Phil Okwedy for great conversation and common interest.

Alison Anderson for introducing me to Stagville.

In Search of Fanny the Barmaid

Quotes
O'Neill, Eugene G., Bound East for Cardiff, in *The Provincetown Plays, First Series* (New York: Frank Shay, 1916).

References
Allo, Samuel, *Stonewaller,* oral tale.

Bottomless Hole, oral tale.

Stevenson, Peter, 'Crossing the Boundary', *Welsh Folk Tales* (Stroud: The History Press, 2017).

Stevenson, Peter, 'In search of Fanny the barmaid', *Planet the Welsh Internationalist*, No. 225 (Aberystwyth: Planet, Spring 2017).

Stevenson, Peter, 'Tinctured with the Piety of Place', (Curious Travellers, 2016) http://curioustravellers.ac.uk/en/tinctured with-the-piety-of-the-place/

Thanks

Emily Trahair, editor of Planet the Welsh Internationalist, for publishing the first version of Fanny.

Regina Ress for inviting me to share stories at Provincetown Playhouse, Greenwich Village.

Laura Simms and the Center for Engaged Storytelling, New York.

Minister Bob Dayton for his wonderful Welsh puppets and his invitation to perform at the Central Presbyterian Church, Tarentum, Pennsylvania.

Judi Tarowsky for telling West Virginia ghost stories.

The Devil and the Mothman

References

Freeman, Michael, 'Fabula de Beth Kilhart', https://sublime-wales.wordpress.com/attractions/gelerts-grave-at-beddgelert/fabula-de-beth-kelhart

Lyonesse (George Basil Barham), 'The Old Woman Who Fooled the Devil' *Legend Land* (London: Great Western Railway) Vol. 1, 1922.

Mothman Museum, www.mothmanmuseum.com

Stevenson, Peter, *Welsh Folk Tales* (Stroud: The History Press, 2017).

The Flatwoods Monster: A Legacy of Fear (Breedlove, Seth) 2018 [Film].

'Welsh in Kanawha Valley', ohiocambrian.llgc.org.uk/tudalen.html?file=CAM0014&tudalen=CAM24&lng=en

Thanks
Mark and Josie for the goat-free road trip.
Michael Freeman for his tireless research.
Rachel Chalmers and DURESS forfunding the Hafod Project.
Judi Tarowsky for the New York couple in Flatwoods.

Owl-Women and Eagle-Men

Welsh References

Davies, Jonathan Ceredig, *Folk-lore of West and Mid-Wales* (Aberystwyth: Welsh Gazette, 1911).

Davies, Sioned, trans., 'Blodeuwedd', *The Mabinogion* (Oxford: University Press, 2007).

Davies, Sioned, trans., 'Manawydan', *The Mabinogion* (Oxford: University Press, 2007).

Evans, Myra, *Casgliad o Chwedlau Newydd* (Aberystwyth: Cambrian News, 1926).

Gruffydd, Eirlys, *Gwrachod Cymru Ddoe a Heddiw* (Llanrwst, Gwasg Carreg Gwalch, 1988).

Gwyndaf, Robin, *Welsh Folk Tales/Chwedlau Gwerin Cymru* (Cardiff: National Museum of Wales, 1989).

Lewes, Mary, 'Witchcraft and Wizardry in Wales', *The Queer Side of Things* (London, Selwyn & Blount, 1923).

Owen, Elias, *Welsh Folk-lore: a Collection of the Folk Tales and Legends of North Wales* (Oswestry: Woodall Minshall & Co, 1896).

Radford, Ken, *Tales of North Wales*, (London: Skilton & Shaw, 1982) pp. 100–101.

Rhys, Sir John, *Celtic Folklore: Welsh and Manx,* Vol. 1 (Oxford: Henry Frowde, 1891).

Stevenson, Peter, *Welsh Folk Tales* (Stroud: The History Press, 2017).

Suggett, Richard, *A History of Magic and Witchcraft in Wales* (Stroud: The History Press, 2008).

•◆•

The stories of Sarah Thorne of Bunner Flats, Ma Heaton, Old Lady Harris, Zubkinka Lovac and Martha Pringle, are from: Musick, Ruth Ann, 'Wisdom and Witchery in West Virginia Folklore', *Traditions: a Journal of West Virginia Folk Culture* (Fairmont WV, 2015).

Appalachian References

Cavender, Anthony, *Folk Medicine in Southern Appalachia* (Chapel Hill: University of North Carolina, 2003).

Erenow, 'Big Trouble at Booger Hollow', https://erenow.com/common/america-bewitched/37.php

Gainer, Patrick, *Witches Ghosts and Signs, Folklore of the Southern Appalachians* (Morgantown: West Virginia University Press, 1975).

Mooney, James, *Myths of the Cherokee* (USA, 1902).

McNeil, WK ed., *Appalachian Images in Folk and Popular Culture* (Knoxville: University of Tennessee 1995 2nd ed).

Nester, Sarah Smith, 'Women in the Appalachian Home' www.smliv.com/features/women-in-the-appalachian-home

Pompey, Sherman Lee, *Granny Gore's Ozark Folk Medicine* (Author, 1961).

Teuton, Christopher B., *The Turtle Island Liars' Club* (University of North Carolina Press, 2012).

Ward, Beth, 'The Long Tradition of Folk Healing Among Southern Appalachian Women', https://www.atlasobscura.com/articles/southern-appalachia-folk-healers-granny-women-neighbor-ladies

Wess, Anna, 'The Last of the Granny Witches', https://appalachianink.net/2015/09/06/the-last-of-the-granny-witches

Thanks

West Virginia Folklife Center, Fairmont State University.

Special Thanks

Curers, Charms, and Curses / Meddygon, Swynion, a Melltithion:
Monongalia Arts Center, Morgantown, West Virginia
Artists Valériane Leblond, Zoe Childerley, Maria Hayes, Jacob
Whittaker, Ruth Jên Evans, Veronika Derkova and Sian Bowman.
Amgueddfa Ceredigion Museum.
Morgantown History Museum.
The Moon-eyed People and the White Ravens, first performed
March 2018: Canolfan Celfyddydau. Aberystwyth Arts Centre.
Ailsa Mair Hughes for the music and songs.
Croesi'r Terfynnau/Crossing the Boundary, 'first performed Jan
2017, with Ailsa Mair Hughes: Llyfrgell Genedlaethol Cymru/
National Library of Wales.
George Ewart Evans Centre
for Storytelling, 'Storytelling and Place'
Symposium, April 2017.
Helen Edwards, for
proofreading.

Society *for*
Storytelling

Since 1993, The Society for Storytelling has championed the ancient art of oral storytelling and its long and honourable history – not just as entertainment, but also in education, health, and inspiring and changing lives. Storytellers, enthusiasts and academics support and are supported by this registered charity to ensure the art is nurtured and developed throughout the UK.

Many activities of the Society are available to all, such as locating storytellers on the Society website, taking part in our annual National Storytelling Week at the start of every February, purchasing our quarterly magazine Storylines, or attending our Annual Gathering – a chance to revel in engaging performances, inspiring workshops, and the company of like-minded people.

You can also become a member of the Society to support the work we do. In return, you receive free access to Storylines, discounted tickets to the Annual Gathering and other storytelling events, the opportunity to join our mentorship scheme for new storytellers, and more. Among our great deals for members is a 30% discount off titles from The History Press.

For more information, including how to join, please visit

www.sfs.org.uk

First published 2019
Reprinted 2022

The History Press
97 St George's Place,
Cheltenham, Gloucestershire, GL50 3QB
www.thehistorypress.co.uk

British Library Cataloguing in Publication Data.
A catalogue record for this book is available from the British Library.

ISBN 978 0 7509 9142 1

Typesetting and origination by The History Press
Printed by TJ Books Limited, Padstow, Cornwall

MIX
Paper | Supporting
responsible forestry
FSC
www.fsc.org   FSC® C013056

The Moon-Eyed People

Folk Tales from Welsh America

Peter Stevenson

Dedicated to the Kemps of West Virginia
and the Andersons of North Carolina